Praise for Lainey Reese's
Damaged Goods

"The sex in the book is fun and extremely hot."

~ *Fiction Vixen*

"If you are looking for a read that keeps your temp running hot, this is for you. Ms. Reese loads her stories with the sexiest men and women, then adds the perfect amount of kink to keep everything interesting."

~ *Coffee Time Romance & More*

"While the sex and BDSM scenes are plentiful, there is a lot more to this book than sex. [...] Lainey is a gifted writer with a knack for writing characters with a great balance of depth, strength, and emotion."

~ *Guilty Pleasures Book Reviews*

Look for these titles by
Lainey Reese

Now Available:

Snowfall

New York
A Table for Three
Damaged Goods

Damaged Goods

Lainey Reese

SAMHAIN
PUBLISHING

Samhain Publishing, Ltd.
11821 Mason Montgomery Road, 4B
Cincinnati, OH 45249
www.samhainpublishing.com

Damaged Goods
Print ISBN: 978-1-61921-269-5
Digital ISBN: 978-1-60928-970-6

Editing by Amy Sherwood
Cover by Kendra Egert

First Samhain Publishing, Ltd. electronic publication: August 2012
First Samhain Publishing, Ltd. print publication: July 2013

Dedication

This book is dedicated to my friends and co-workers at my day job. Amber, Katie, Angie, Barb and Jenny: you have all been so amazing and supportive of me. You all make me feel important and special every day. Even though we work in a conservative place of business, none of you ever make me feel like I should keep my "spicy" writing a secret. In fact you all go out of your way to tell our customers and brag on me. You make me feel loved and grateful to be there. I don't know what I did to be lucky enough to end up where I did, but I'm thankful for it and thankful for you all. I love each and every one of you.

Chapter One

The slut is dead! After all she did to everyone who ever met her, it's a surprise we're not having a party instead of this stupid funeral. Look at them all, crying. I wonder if they hated her as much as I did. Maybe they're just faking it. She was a spiteful, money-hungry slut, and I'm glad she's dead. I only wish she had suffered. I only wish that stupid bitch had seen it coming! I only wish I could kill her again.

Fatigue was burning a fiery crater through Brice Marshall's brain. It was eleven o'clock on a Friday night, and here he was, hunched over crime scene photos, breathing the stale air of the detective's den and trying to kill himself with microwaved coffee that was at least twelve hours old.

"Kent," he muttered to his partner, who was seated at the desk facing his and looked just as bad as Brice felt. "It's here. It's always here. Why can't we see it?" In a rare show of frustration, Brice shoved the file and photos to the floor. "Five days, Kent. Five fucking days and we've got nothing. Five days ago, someone hacked that poor kid to shit and we've been running around with our heads up our asses."

"Mmmhmm," was all the response Brandon Kent gave. He knew they'd been killing themselves looking into this. They hadn't worked less than a sixteen-hour day since they got the first call.

They were good at what they did. They had the highest arrest rate in the precinct, and this wasn't the only case they had on their plate. There were three other ongoing investigations that needed their attention and time. This one was eating at them like a cancer, though, and Kent knew one of them was going to have to call it. The case would never be over until there was an arrest. But when they had no leads or direction to follow, they were going to have to shift focus to a case that they had a better chance at solving while the trail was still hot.

"As much as it tears out my guts to say this," Kent wearily began, "we may just have to tap out on this one."

He almost didn't move in time to miss the empty coffee mug that Brice chucked at his head. "Hey! Watch it!" he shouted. "I don't want that any more than you. You know that! But it's like you said—it's been five fucking days and we got dick on this one."

He held up one hand and started folding the fingers under one at a time with his other as he spoke. "We got no weapon." Down went the thumb. "We got no fingerprints." Down went the pointer finger. "We got no witnesses." Down went the ring finger. "And we got no fucking clue as to a motive." Down went the pinky, and he was left flipping Brice off as he said, "So fuck you and your coffee cup!"

Brice stared at his partner through bleary eyes. He knew that what Kent said was reasonable. He knew that he was right. It didn't make it any easier to swallow. "I can't, buddy. Not on this one. I don't know what it is, but I can't look at her and walk away. She's mine. She's been mine from the first."

Brice looked down at the pile on the floor and thought it was fitting that the only two pieces of papers from the whole stack that weren't upside down or obscured were photos of her. Amber Calkins smiled up at him from one with impossibly bright blue eyes, a sassy bob of glossy brown hair and a flirty little wrinkle on her pert nose. The picture was taken at a beach with the blue of the ocean surrounding her as she laughed into the camera. She looked fresh and vibrant and like she knew she had the world at her feet.

The other photo was from the crime scene. That lovely face with all its spunk and charm was mashed into a pile of filthy garbage. Blood-soaked clothes clung to what had been a great figure. Her arms and legs were outstretched. Either she hadn't had time to try and block her fall or she'd already been dead before she fell. More of her blood saturated the garbage she lay upon; it had poured out of her slender frame like a flood to surround her in red the way the ocean had surrounded her in blue in the other photo. Over fifty stab wounds covered that tiny back. It didn't seem possible that that many could fit in such a small space, but there they were. Her back had been reduced to what sickeningly resembled ground beef and Brice, a hardened homicide detective with over ten years on the force, hadn't had a burger since.

From everything they'd been able to learn about her, she was a bright, good-natured and big-hearted twenty-year-old who liked driving her sporty car, buying ridiculous clothes for her ridiculous excuse of a miniature dog and working at the Surf-N-Slurp, one of those places where mostly twenty-somethings hung out to drink designer coffee and surf the web on the free Wi-Fi. Everybody liked her—even the boys whose hearts she'd broken hadn't had anything bad to say about her—and nobody had any idea why someone would want her dead.

But someone hadn't liked her. And someone had wanted her dead badly enough to stab her fifty times. That told them one thing—it was personal. It took an amazing amount of strength to do this, and stamina, the kind of stamina that only deep-seated hatred could provide.

"I know, man," Kent said. "I know. But what about the Parker case? Or Dillon? Both those still need a lot of legwork, and I can't believe I have to even tell you that. Look, we're not getting anything done tonight. So let's call it a day and head home."

With ill grace, Brice gave in and, after putting his desk into something close to order, followed Kent out the door.

Chapter Two

Brice wasn't in the mood to face his place. It was a nice set-up in a decent part of town, but it was also empty. He didn't even have a ridiculous excuse of a miniature dog waiting for him. Just a dying plant that one of his sisters had given him and a fridge full of rotting leftover takeout.

Without reasoning the why of it, he headed for his cousin's place. The restaurant was sure to be booked to capacity, but he was feeling just shitty enough to play the family card to get himself in. After a late dinner and a stiff drink, he thought he might just head to the restaurant's connected nightclub and see if there was someone there who would make the empty apartment seem a little less empty. Even if it was just for the night.

"Detective Marshall!" Mike exclaimed once he spotted Brice walk into the lobby. "I didn't know you would be here tonight! This is great!" Mike took hold of Brice's hand and continued to shake it vigorously as he smiled up at the taller man. "I didn't see your name on the reserved list or I would have saved you the private table."

"Don't worry about that." Brice's smile was more of a grimace and didn't fool Mike for a second. "I don't have a reservation. I know you guys'll be booked solid, but can you squeeze me out a corner somewhere? I just need a meal that doesn't come from a rolling cart or packaged in Styrofoam."

Brice must have looked like he felt, because Mike didn't hesitate. "Hey, boss man has rules," he said as he led Brice toward a back corner table that was reserved for overbooking or when VIPs showed up unannounced. In this establishment, VIP was quite literally VIP—only top-ranking entertainers and politicians got this table. No B-list actors or self-absorbed heiresses got the treatment here, and definitely not just any cop off the street.

Mike added as he handed over a menu, "Boss has rules, and even if a Rockefeller walked in right now, he would give you this table."

Brice wasn't in his seat more than five minutes before a curvy little brunette slid into the chair across from his. She smiled up at him, blinked her big dark eyes and Brice knew two things—there was a God, and He was a man.

"Hey, gorgeous," he said. "Wanna run away with me?"

She leaned across the table and laid a soft kiss on his cheek. "You know my heart's going to break the day you stop asking me that." Her smile was as tender as the hand she laid over his when she asked, "Brice, what's wrong? "

Brice smiled and gave her hand a good squeeze. "Nothing I can't fix. Where are those men of yours? I thought they imploded whenever you were more than three feet away."

Reassured by his genuine smile and the teasing, Riley replied, "Oh, I'm working on widening the radius. I can get up to ten now before the alarms start going off."

Just then, Kincade Marshall came up behind Riley's chair and slid his hands along the tops of her shoulders. "Personally, I think she only tests those boundaries because she enjoys the repercussions."

With the last word, his hands slid up from her shoulders to encircle her fragile neck. Brice watched without any fear for her, knowing that his cousin would cut off those hands himself before he'd ever hurt her. It took only a second before Riley's breath got shallow and her cheeks flushed as his cousin tightened his grip. When her back arched, Brice saw that her nipples were hard under her dress.

"I believe you're right, Cade." Brice deliberately focused on her breasts as he spoke to his cousin. "Her pretty nipples are hard. When was the last time you tanned that juicy ass of hers?" At Riley's whimper, Brice's gaze darted up to meet hers. He grinned at the look of both panic and anticipation on her face.

Riley tried to sound calm when she said, "Brice, for God's sake, don't encourage him. He'll be trying to make me come right here in this seat if you do."

Cade looked as if he could get behind that idea, but Brice took pity on her. "C'mon, Cade. Sit down and buy me a drink. You can torment your wife any time, and I haven't seen you in a month."

Cade first tilted Riley's chin until she was looking up at him. "My sweet. Tell me before you go walking off, even in the restaurant."

When he saw that Riley was about to argue, Cade tightened his grip even more, knowing just how much pressure to apply before it became pain. It dilated her lovely eyes with pleasure and earned him a compliant nod of submission. Then he sat next to her and placed one hand on her thigh.

Brice could tell by her sudden frozen posture that his cousin's touch must be very high up on her leg. He guessed that the slightest movement would bring his fingers to where she was probably already wet and ready for him. Brice knew she wouldn't move, though. She would wait—as she'd been lovingly taught over the last two years—until given the command. As a submissive, she was a dominant's wet dream come true.

"Hey! Why didn't I know you'd be here?" Trevor Wellington swooped in and delivered a solid punch to Brice's shoulder, his version of a hug. Then he leaned over and kissed Riley. Not just a quick peck, but a full, open-mouthed, tongue-thrusting kiss that had Riley panting and all but melting in her seat. He pulled back with obvious reluctance and sat in the one remaining chair.

Brice looked at the three of them and thought that no matter how unconventional their relationship was, it sure worked for them. Two years ago, they had committed themselves to each other in a garden ceremony at the Marshalls' summer home, and the three of them were as blissful now as they were then. They showed no signs of slowing down.

"You didn't know because I didn't know." Brice sighed and settled in. For the first time in five days, he allowed himself to relax. "I drove here on autopilot. I think I was headed home for leftover Chinese, but when I stopped the car I was here instead."

"Awful late to be having dinner." Cade's stare took in all the details. Brice thought Cade could probably see the fatigue and the stress he was wearing as plain as he saw the clothes on his back. "Why don't we have dinner brought up so you can fill us in and crash after?"

"Well, as nice as that sounds, I was thinking about flexing my charm muscles in the club after dinner. Maybe find my own Riley for the night."

Riley snorted inelegantly. "Brice. I swear, you can do a lot better than a"—finger quotes—"Riley."

"No, he can't." This was spoken in unison by both Cade and Trevor.

Riley waved that off with an eye roll. "Seriously. All you are going to meet there is a quick, cheap thrill. You need a decent girl who's going to love you and hmmphh." Trevor's hand over her mouth saved Brice from having to listen to the rest.

"Little One," Trevor whispered, "don't you remember where Cade found you?" Riley's blush was instant and bright as flame.

"Yes," she whispered back, and then she rallied. "But! I was new in town, and I had no idea what I was getting myself into when I came here. And! I thought it was only going to be a wild fling once I did realize it." Her chin thrust up, and there was fire in her eyes as she faced off with Trevor and dared him to say different.

Before Trevor responded and the debate got into full swing, Brice spoke. "Riley, much as I appreciate your concern, 'quick cheap thrill' is exactly what I was hoping for tonight."

"Oh." Riley's voice fairly dripped with disappointment. Despite her very unconventional relationship, she still was a traditional girl and felt Brice should settle down. "You know, there is this lovely girl at the center that I've been getting really close to. She just started about eight months ago and she's so cute and sweet and hmphh." This time Cade's hand saved Brice.

"No, Ry," he said. "No matchmaking. This is my favorite cousin, and I won't have him terrified that every time he comes around you'll have a woman waiting to pounce."

"Thanks for the offer." Brice smiled. "I'll let you know when I'm ready for the fairy-tale ending to my bachelorhood."

"Seriously, Brice," Cade said, obviously not wanting to leave him on his own in the condition he was in. "Why don't you join us? If not tonight, then soon. It's been several months since we last had the pleasure, and I think you're right, Riley *does* need a spanking."

The air around the table got heavy with silence while Cade stared at Riley, Trevor looked to Brice, and Brice and Riley locked gazes. Brice knew that the three of them were a solid unbreakable unit, and the lines there were clearly drawn. They were, however, definitely of the BDSM lifestyle, and part of that lifestyle included exhibition. He also knew that he was the only person the men trusted enough to indulge in that with. Every time they offered it left him humbled and aroused. Although the club had a special section just for BDSM, his cousin and Trevor rarely took Riley there. They preferred to keep her to themselves.

As a waitress set a plate of mouthwatering food in front of him, Brice considered their offer.

He seldom got to indulge that part of himself. Quick cheap thrills were not the environment for BDSM play because, contrary to popular belief, it was all about trust. Nobody trusted someone they'd only hooked up with for an hour.

However, as he ate his dinner and caught up on family news, he thought tonight he was going to get everything he could out of that one hour and hope it would be enough.

Chapter Three

Brice strode out past the bar and headed for the dance floor as soon as he entered the club. It was packed tight with people pressing in all around him. Like a laser, he focused on a curvy blonde at the edge of the dancers. She was barely clothed in a halter-top that draped in the front and was only held together in the back by two small gold chains. What passed for her skirt flashed the smooth, round cheeks of her ass every time she moved. For what he had in mind, she was perfect.

The music was a primal beat that fueled the fever raging in his blood. He pushed past one couple dancing so close it was hard to tell whose limbs were whose. He stumbled when another couple backed into him. He shoved the man back without taking his eyes off his target. Then a slender redhead drifted in and out of his line of sight.

He'd always been a sucker for red hair, and it never even registered to him that he'd automatically changed directions as soon as he saw her. Brice was like a cat on the hunt and new, more tempting prey had been sighted. He closed in like the predator he was. A smile of unabashed delight spread across his face when she left the dance floor and headed for the club's private playrooms.

Two beefy bodyguards stood on either side of the entrance. They nodded politely to Brice's target, and she passed into the darkened hallway without slowing. A man with a shaved and tattooed head tried to pass next and was stopped by the guard on the left. Brice didn't wait to see the outcome, just nodded to the other guard and walked right in.

The playrooms in the club were a whole different world from the club. Brice often thought that if the club were a body, the playrooms would be its heart. In the playrooms people were stripped down to the basic primal animal. No pretense, no façade, no fronts. Everyone here came for sex, unapologetically seeking what the body craved. Whether Dom, sub, voyeur or anything in between, this was the place where that part of someone thrived.

The chaos and noise from the dance area faded to a distant hum as he neared the lounge. In this section, the music was low and instrumental. The seating here was primarily sofas and deep, overstuffed chairs. There was a long mahogany bar along the back wall and behind it, instead of the traditional display of bottles, there was a display of a different sort.

A woman was tied standing spread-eagle on a rotating platform. She was blindfolded and naked. There were red marks from a recent flogging on her breasts and thighs. Brice guessed she must have taken her flogging well, because her Dom was currently kneeling between her legs, eating her to a screaming climax. As it peaked, the small crowd at the bar gave murmurs of encouragement and cheers, obviously appreciating the show.

Brice paid them little attention, his focus still on his target. She headed straight for the main desk, and he hung back to see what she would check in as. In this section of the club, safety was king, and it was members-only. Every person who joined had to pass a strict screening that included background checks, a psych evaluation and a clean medical screening, the last of which had to be renewed every three months.

The check-in area looked a lot like a coat check you'd find in most any high-end restaurant. In a way, it was. Subs and Doms alike turned in all personal items there to be picked up when they left. What was different about this coat check was when you traded in your belongings you got either a collar or an armband instead of a ticket stub. Doms got armbands, subs got a collar.

Brice relaxed and leaned against the doorframe while he waited as the slender redhead traded in her sparkling gold bag. He couldn't have been more thrilled when the young woman behind the counter handed back a collar.

"Why is this one yellow?" he heard her ask.

"Because you're not a first timer anymore," Brice answered from where he stood. She jumped and turned to him, and Brice got a look at her from the front for the first time.

She had eyes that seemed to swallow up her heart-shaped face. They were as green as spring grass, and Brice took a moment to admire their beauty before he went on. Her features were delicate, with a small nose, high cheekbones and a slight dimple in her slightly rounded chin. She had a luscious mouth that was painted a glossy peach, and he wanted nothing more than to take a bite. He'd already noticed that she was taller than average and slender, and now he saw that although slim, she was not lacking in curves.

"The red collar is only for a sub's first three visits. I take it this is your fourth visit?" He didn't need her nod or the, "Yes it is, Master Brice" from Candy, the check-in girl, to let him know he was right. It was all there in her expression.

He kept his eyes on her as he stepped forward and walked behind the counter. A quick look at the collar clutched in her hands assured him she wasn't already taken. A claimed sub had cuffs attached to her collar, or at least a chain. This one had neither. With a nod to Candy conveying she should keep an eye on the sub for him, he went to stow his things and get his band.

He wasn't gone for a minute, but he was still impressed that she hadn't moved at all while waiting. It boded well for what he had in mind. Her eyes fixated on the black band he now had on his bicep as he rounded the counter and approached her.

"Eyes down, sub," he said as he took the collar from her fingers and clasped it on her slender neck. When she instinctively tried to step back and didn't lower her eyes, he gathered the hair at her nape and held tight. He applied stronger and stronger pressure until she gave a small gasp and arched into his grip. "I know you are new, but even with only three nights here, you would have been taught the basics." He watched her for signs of reluctance or discomfort as she struggled to obey him.

What he saw was a strong, independent young woman who was having trouble coming to terms with the submissive side of her nature. Her pupils were dilated, there was a flush in her cheeks and her lips were parted and moist. All signs that she was aroused by what was happening. She also had her fists clenched and her eyebrows wrinkled in a frown. That showed him that she was not quite comfortable with the knowledge that this was exciting her.

It was just the combination of emotions that a Dom found irresistible. At least a Dom like him. Here was a woman who had a whole world of discovery ahead of her. The thought of all the firsts that she had yet to experience was a heady rush.

"You know," he said in a mild voice, "there are Doms out there who like subs already trained and broken in. Subs who know the rules and will bend and yield to their Will readily and easily." He smiled and tightened his grip on her hair. "I am not that kind of Dom."

Terryn gulped and tried not to squeak. This guy was seriously hot. He had to be over six feet, with dark hair, chocolate-brown eyes and a great face. It was classic, she thought, and so beautifully male it made her think of men like Cary Grant and Rock Hudson, back when tall, dark and handsome was really tall and dark and handsome.

Here he was, movie-star perfect, and he was a Master. A Master who had her by the hair. Terryn wondered if maybe she was home in bed, because this had to be a dream.

"Um." Terryn wasn't sure if she was allowed to speak or not, but she risked it. "I have had some training." He quirked an eyebrow at her in an expression that spoke volumes, and she finally lowered her eyes and added, "Sir. Um, Master?" Something in her chest warmed when he chuckled and released her hair.

"Come with me, little sub, and you can tell me just what kind of training you've had so far." He turned and walked toward the lounge area.

She risked a quick look at Candy, who'd been very helpful and nice on her previous visits. Candy gave her a smile and thumbs-up that Terryn decided was approval of the Dom. Then she hurried after him, with eyes down. She only lowered them as far as it took to watch the way the muscles in his rear moved and flexed as he walked. The man had one fine rearview.

"Sub." Terryn jumped in surprise when he spoke over his shoulder, "Eyes on the floor."

With a guilty blush that she felt staining her cheeks, she peeked up to see him watching her through one of the mirrors on the wall. "Oops," she said, and this time lowered her eyes all the way and followed him to a deep burgundy chair.

The chair was plush and inviting and looked big enough to hold a family of four...until he sat in it. All of a sudden, there wasn't enough room for her. He was solidly built, and he sat sprawled in the middle of the chair with his legs stretched out. The position left only inches on either side of him to spare.

Terryn took a deep breath. This is what she wanted. This is what she was looking for. She'd been reading about the D/s lifestyle for months, and now it was happening. She took a deep breath, wrestled her inner feminist to the ground and knelt at his feet.

It was harder than she thought it would be. That inner feminist was screeching at her to get up off the floor, she wasn't a dog, and the harder she tried to ignore that voice, the louder it got. But she stayed. She remembered her reading and her first couple visits and spread her knees wide, then brought her hands to rest, palms up on her thighs.

Her Dom didn't say a word as she knelt there. She was keeping her eyes down, so she could not see his face, but she knew he was watching her. She felt it. As she concentrated on that, on his attention, that voice eventually faded until she couldn't hear it anymore. She became solely focused outside herself and whether or not he was pleased.

Just when she was going to risk a look, she felt his hand on her hair. He stroked softly along the curls and then he gathered them up and off to one shoulder. His fingers lightly caressed her neck above the collar, then he traced circles over the shell of her ear. Goose bumps chased up and down her back as he continued a tickling path along her check with those blunt, calloused fingertips.

"Is this the first time you've knelt at a Dom's feet?" His voice caused more goose bumps, and Terryn could only nod as she waited for what would happen next. "We've only just met, and I have to assume this is your first unescorted visit here. I would never dream of asking you to trust me this soon. But you've read the rules and you've been through the orientation. You can also look around and see the bodyguards that are here for your protection. Trust that. Trust what you've learned so far and we will stay to the open play areas so you can be assured that the club will keep you safe." He gave her a couple moments to think about that, and the rest of the tension left her.

"You make a pretty picture there at my feet. Pretty enough that I'm the envy of every Dom here tonight. But we need to talk, and I find that talking is better done face-to-face. Come up here." She started to get to her feet, but before she could move, his hands scooped under her arms and he lifted her into his lap as though she weighed less than nothing.

After she was settled with her bottom on the seat on one side of him and her legs on the other, he draped his arms around her waist and asked, "What's your name?"

"Terryn." She kept her eyes down. Only now she did it because she was too embarrassed to look him in the face. Terryn hadn't sat in a man's lap since her last visit to Santa.

"Terryn," he said. "Lovely. How did you discover that you were a submissive?"

Talk about getting right to the point, she thought. "Um. Well. I never have really enjoyed being with men, really," she said, and then stumbled to a halt when she realized how that sounded. "I'm not gay. I mean, I like boys. Um, guys. I mean, men. I like men. But, urgh." With a groan of pure humiliation, she buried her face in her hands and wished fervently that she could slide back onto the floor and then slink away. His chuckle and the warm hand rubbing soothing circles on her back did little to ease her mortification. "This wasn't supposed to be like this."

"Really?" he asked, his voice soft and smooth in her ear. "How was it supposed to be?"

"I've been fantasizing about this moment for months. I've pictured myself with my first real Dom a million different ways, and in those dreams I never stammer like an idiot." With another groan, she crumpled up further and brought her knees up.

Just as she was about to fold into a ball of misery, he turned her face to him with a hand on her chin. He was smiling. She liked his smile. He smiled with his whole face, not just his mouth. There were fine lines in the corner of his eyes that deepened as his whole expression lifted. He had great teeth and lips that were full without looking like they belonged on a girl. Just a simple smile from him, and she felt her spirits lighten.

"Well, your dreams differ from mine, then. As for me, having a beautiful, blushing, redheaded sub cuddled in my lap is right up there on my list of dreams come true." His smile deepened, and that warm place in her chest got warmer and her embarrassment melted under the heat of it. "Now, you were saying that you like men?"

Terryn rallied and tried again. "I like men. It's just that when I was with them it was mostly boring. I mean, sometimes it was good. But for the most part, I just thought there was something wrong with me because I could never..." She was blushing again. Terryn gave herself a mental push and blurted it out. "Come. I could never come and I almost always faked it. 'Cause, I mean, it's not the guy's fault, right? I'd feel sorry for them. They would try, but I just couldn't do it." She let out a big breath and tried very hard to look like she was comfortable having this kind of conversation with a perfect stranger.

"Terryn." His voice was a little deeper now. It had an unmistakably disciplinarian tone to it. "The first rule in this is trust. The D/s balance is delicate, and there has to be complete honesty." His hands tightened on her and his voice got deeper yet. "You will never fake an orgasm again. Are we clear?" Terryn nodded and tried not to squirm.

"Good," he said. "I'm glad we understand each other on that. So, you found vanilla sex boring. What happened to make you look into BDSM instead of, say, swinging or exploring with women?"

"I read a lot. I like romance novels." She waited for him to say something disparaging about chick-lit, and when he remained silent she took encouragement from that and went on, "I noticed a pattern. If the hero of the story was strong and even overbearing, I loved it. The ones where the men were soft and sweet, I couldn't stand." He smiled at that, and she continued, "Seriously, I read one where the man was all flowers and poetry and soft tender love scenes and I thought I was going to puke. Give me a hero who's only two steps up from carrying a club and I can't get enough." He chuckled again and brought one of her hands to his mouth.

As he nibbled on her fingers one at a time, he asked, "So, you thought you'd see if you enjoy a Neanderthal in reality as much as you do in fiction?" He waited until she nodded before he asked, "Who brought you on your first three visits, and why aren't they here for your fourth?"

"A friend of mine is a member. She's also a sub and kind of new to this. She loves it and told me that I wouldn't be sorry. She gave me some hands-on instruction and has been answering all my questions. I lucked out with her because she's been great. My first three visits, it was just the two of us, and we just watched other peoples' scenes so I could see what it was like and make sure I was ready for this. Tonight she brought a date along."

As he leisurely nibbled his way along her palm, it became harder and harder to remember what she was talking about. "We were all dancing in the club area first to get warmed up before we headed back here. They were going to help me find a Dom and then they were going to keep an eye on me. We had agreed that she was going to watch me through my first scene."

Her breath caught as those lips and teeth found a particularly sensitive spot. "Then they decided they wanted privacy instead of the club and left." He raised a brow at that, and Terryn rushed to reassure him before he judged her friend. "I wasn't mad. We all talked about it, and they would have been cool if I wanted them to stay. She really likes this guy, though, and I didn't blame her for wanting to be with him instead of babysitting me." Terryn's voice was softer and softer as she spoke, getting lost in the feel of his mouth on her hand. His tongue was tracing tiny patterns on her palm now.

"I was supposed to leave too." She shrugged when his eyes snapped to her. There was a frown on his face and he nipped hard on the pad of her thumb. "I tried to leave. I was out front waiting for a cab, and I just thought, no. I'm not going to wait any longer. I've been reading and studying and waiting for this for what feels like my whole life. I wasn't going to put it off for even one more night when I didn't have to. So I sent the taxi on its way and marched right back in here."

She smiled at him a little sheepishly and confessed, "I was fine until I saw the yellow collar. Scared me to death. All of the sudden I thought, 'Holy cow! I'm in for it now.' And I was gonna go home after all. Then you walked in."

Terryn smiled at him and let everything she was feeling show on her face. She hoped he could see that she was still scared, but that she was open and ready and glad that he had been there. She also hoped desperately that he would remember this was her first time with a Dom and not go too hard on her.

Chapter Four

Brice watched the emotions drift like currents across her expressive face. He wanted to spank her fool ass for not leaving when her friend did. But he understood—hell, it was like she'd been surviving on bread and water up 'til now, and just when someone had showed her there was a whole banquet out there, they told her she had to wait before she could eat.

He remembered the first time he'd had D/s sex. He had still been in college, and Trevor and Cade told him about a girl who had let them tie her up and both take her at the same time. He'd been so intrigued and turned on by the story that he'd looked up a BDSM club close to campus and went that same night. The club had been seedy and dank, but he'd learned a lot about who he was in that place. If someone had told him to wait and come back later, before he'd had a taste for himself, he would have ignored them too.

But still, he told her, "You should have taken that cab. This club has some safety measures in place, but as a newcomer you are extremely vulnerable." When he saw that she wasn't going to agree, he decided to let it pass. "But I'm personally very glad you didn't, so I'll let it go.

"Now," he continued "I need to know what you've done before and what you want to do. You said you haven't been with anyone in the club, but have you ever tried BDSM with a boyfriend?"

"No."

The answer filled him with what he called his Captain Kirk glee. May not be modern, but it was what it was. He loved going where no man had gone before.

"Ever been tied up or restrained?" When she shook her head, he said, "We'll start there." He scooped one arm under her shoulders and the other under her knees, then stood and headed to the equipment area. Her eyes were opened wide in her anxious face. He could tell she was torn between her fear of biting off more than she could chew and excitement over what was about to happen.

He spoke to her as he set her on her feet in front of a St. Andrew's cross, "We are just going to try restraints for now. I want to see how you react to that before we take it any further. Tell me, have you already decided on a safe word?"

She nodded and said the last thing he could have imagined. "Pickles."

The ridiculous choice made him laugh and he made a mental note to himself to find out later why she chose it. He saw that her breathing had increased, and she was back to clenching her fists. "Terryn," he said softly, and ran a finger along her collar. "Tell me why you have a yellow collar."

She swallowed and gave him a look before answering, "Because I'm not new anymore."

"That's a start. Go on."

"What do you mean?"

"Tell me why the collars are colored and what the colors mean. I need to know how much you know."

"Oh." She looked like she'd just been given a pop quiz. "The red is only for your first couple visits. The yellow is for after that, and then you get a green one."

"And what do those colors represent?" he asked while slowly running his hands up and down her bare arms.

"Um, the red one means that no one can touch you, you're still learning, and the yellow means you're ready to try. The green means you're up for grabs."

He slowly shook his head and lifted first one of her arms and then the next into its restraint. "Not exactly. The yellow tells the Dom to be cautious, go slow and don't assume this sub knows everything she should. The green tells him this sub is confident and knows what the rules are. That allows him to go forward without having to break character, so to speak."

Both her arms were secure now, and he knelt down to place her feet. As he positioned each one in turn, he removed her shoes. Heels may do wonders for a woman's legs, but for him nothing was sexier than bare feet during a scene.

The restraints were leather. Lined with thick cotton, they safeguarded against injury. Even so, he checked the fit on all four before standing back. "Any collar, even a green one, doesn't mean a sub is up for grabs. The sub always has the true power. Did you know that?" His eyes wandered over her slowly, from her bare spread feet to the tips of her widespread fingers.

When he met her fascinated gaze, she shook her head and said in a whisper, "How could this be power? I'm trapped. You could do anything right now." From the look on her face, he could tell that thought was equally arousing and frightening to her.

"Ah, I could, huh?" He stepped close, until his chest was against her breasts and his lips brushed her cheek as he spoke. "I could flog you?" She caught her breath and held it. "Or perhaps I could strip you and share you with some of the men watching from the bar?" Her head whipped around to stare in horror at the bar and the people who were watching them instead of the show going on behind the bartender. "Wait, I've got a better idea—how about I just lift this charming dress out of my way and fuck you where you stand?" He slid a palm up one perfect, trembling thigh, and just as he was expecting, as soon as he reached the hem of her gold skirt, she panicked.

"No! Pickles! Pickles!" Every muscle in her body strained against the bindings. Before the words had even left her lips, he was two feet away from her with his hands up in front of him. For a moment, she still looked frightened, and then the fear gave way to understanding.

When he was sure she was no longer scared, he stepped back into position. "The sub always has the ultimate power, because with one word, no matter how ridiculous that word may be, she can stop everything."

He brought his hands up where she could see them and slowly lowered them until they were on her waist. "It's a dance, Terryn," he said and took a nip at her earlobe.

"A dance on a high wire suspended over shark-infested waters. I have to know how far to push." His hands slid up and cupped both breasts. "Where you like to be touched." His thumbs feathered across nipples that turned hard as granite.

"And just how much pain is pleasure to you." He pinched down on the hardened tips and felt like a rock star when she arched and let out a cry. "Mmmm, that was a nice sound," he praised. "Can I make it happen again?"

With his thumbs and forefingers, he grasped her nipples and tugged until her breasts were lifted and elongated. Then he pulled in small, forceful pulses. Watching her face for signs of true pain was necessary, but she only arched and panted for him.

He pulled a little harder and—"Ahhh, there it is." He let up and leaned down to lay a kiss on her cheek. "I do love that sound." Then he stepped back and reached for the zipper he'd felt hidden in the side seam of her dress. "This gold color looks amazing on you, but for a sub, you are extremely overdressed."

The silky gold material loosened as the zipper lowered. It was a strapless number, and in a matter of seconds he dropped it at her feet. The throbbing pressure in his cock turned critical as every cell in his body reacted to sight in front of him.

Her red hair blazed in the glow of the lights, surrounding her face in waves of flame. Her arms and legs were stretched, and he could make out the supple musculature in each mouthwatering limb. She was slender and toned, with a gentle flare to her hips. The strapless black bra she had on barely covered her nipples, and he could see them clearly outlined in their delicate covering. The matching panties were those micro style kind that never failed to make his mouth water, just a couple of strings and a triangle of satin. Just above a tiny satin bow where the string met the crotch panel, something caught his eye, and he knelt down for a better look.

"Is that what I think it is?" Her face turned the brightest shade yet, and with one finger he moved the panty aside so he could see. A tattoo of a cartoon bear no bigger than his thumbprint sat just on the edge of delicate red curls.

He leaned forward for a closer look, and she whispered, "It's Winnie the Pooh." When he brought the panties lower and saw what she had on the opposite corner of those curls, she added, "And his honey pot."

Sure enough, across from Pooh was a honey pot lying on its side with honey pouring out of it in a tiny splash that disappeared into the curls below. Both were small and well done. He wasn't a man who normally liked tattoos. If a woman was going to be marked, he preferred to do the marking and to have those marks fade so he could do them again. But these... "Clever, whimsical and just a little bit naughty. Was this your design?" he asked without looking up.

"Um." She cleared her throat and had to take a deep breath before she could talk. He wondered if it was embarrassment or if having him staring so intently at her honey pot was to blame. "It was mine. I was eighteen and thought it'd be flirty. Now I just get embarrassed whenever a man sees them."

He looked up at her, but stayed where he was. "Why?"

"Because, I thought they'd make me more mature and daring. But, hello, it's Winnie the Pooh. Now whenever someone sees them, I feel like a little kid."

"Well," Brice said, looking back at the tattoos, "I like them and think they have just the right amount of daring." He flicked a look up at her with a raised brow and a pirate's grin. "It's daring me to have a taste for myself and see how far down that honey has spilled."

Then he lowered his head, swirled his tongue around the honey pot and followed that splashing trail. When he reached the point where curls gave way to the delicate pink folds of flesh, he eased back. Her panties were dainty and sexy as hell, but they were in his way.

"I'll buy you a new pair," was all he said and then snapped them from her hips with one firm yank. Her gasp and whimper was the perfect soundtrack to accompany what would come next. She was already open thanks to the restraints. Her pubic hair was close-trimmed and didn't cover the fragile lips of her sex. They were stretched wide and glistening. Her clit was slightly enlarged from the little they had done so far, and Brice was determined to see it swell even more before he was through.

"Such a pretty little pussy you have here, Terryn," he complimented. He ran one thick finger around the edge of her inner labia, tracing a teasing arch over her clit without actually touching it. "What do you call it?"

"M-my..." She squirmed when he hit a particularly good spot, then sighed, "My g-g."

He shook his head slowly as he continued to circle and trace the tiny part of her that was growing more plump and damp by the second. "Such a silly name for such an important thing." He rubbed harder, still only grazing one side and then the other of that sensitive bundle of nerves, and he could see she struggled not to beg. "G-g is what a little girl would have. Not a beautiful woman. This lovely, glistening flesh should have a name that matches it."

He traced lower now and found her core melting with juice and heat. It coated the two fingers he used to circle her opening and then slide back between the cheeks of her ass. When the muscles there tensed in shock, he deliberately circled her rim before sliding back to stroke and lightly pinch her outer lips.

"I like pussy. Or core. Or, if I'm feeling especially barbaric, I will call it your cunt. I like the word cunt—it's raw and carnal. It makes me think of all the raw and carnal things I want to do to it."

Terryn whimpered, and Brice felt a shudder go through her. Her clit was so engorged now he knew that it would take very little to bring her to orgasm. He marveled that the men from her past had trouble satisfying such a responsive woman.

He blew on it lightly, and Terryn's whimpers turned to a moan. He drenched one fingertip in the nectar all but dripping from her and slid it slowly and firmly right up to her clit. She squeaked. He again rubbed first one side then the next, careful not to rub over the crest of it, lest she come too quickly. Her leg muscles started to quiver. Next he leaned forward and did the same thing with his tongue. Gone were the whimpers—now she groaned.

It was a mistake. He'd wanted to tease her more. He'd wanted to make her first time in restraints a long, sweaty affair that she would always remember. One taste of her, however, and he knew wouldn't stop. She was slick with arousal, and her velvety flesh felt like heaven under his tongue. With a growl, he forgot his intentions and sucked the pearl of her clitoris into his mouth. He laved it like his favorite piece of hard candy, then thought he'd go mad when she screamed and started climaxing right then.

He didn't let up, didn't think it was possible to at this point. He needed more and angled lower to fuck her with his tongue. She bucked again in her restraints, her screams escalating while his tongue danced in and out of her. With both hands, he reached for the globes of her ass and, with another primal growl, pulled her tight to his face. He wanted to drown in her. He wanted to gorge himself on her until his body was covered with her juice. With a wail that fired up every neuron in his brain, she came again.

Slowly, he stood up, so he could suck and bite and lick his way up her delectable body inch by inch. When he got to her still-covered breasts, he shoved the offending material down with a snarl and sucked one pebbled nipple into his mouth. At the same time, he slid two thick fingers into her still-fluttering sheath. The combined actions set off another piercing orgasm in her, and Brice felt ten fucking feet tall. He pumped hard with his hand, barely remembering to be careful not to hurt her in his passion. After an eternity, he released her breast with a last soft bite and stood to his full height.

He kept his hand lodged deep and flexing as her core continued to pulse around his fingers. He looked into her glazed, unfocused eyes and asked, "Is this what you hoped for?" He leaned down and licked his tongue into her open and panting mouth. "Does this live up to your dreams?"

Another lick, then he sucked her plump bottom lip into his mouth and bit down just hard enough to make her gasp. It also made her pussy clench on his fingers. "God, sweetheart, I could keep you like this forever."

She pleased him right down to the ground when she moaned, "Yes, please," and nodded her head.

"I wanna fuck you, Terryn. I wanna fuck you right here and now. I want to fuck you while you're spread and ready for me. If you aren't ready for that, say pickles now. If you don't, I'm going to fuck you hard and fast and I won't stop until you're begging."

Her glazed eyes slowly came into focus and he saw her try to concentrate. He made himself stop moving. He couldn't quite bring himself to dislodge his fingers or step back—he was only a man, after all—but he held still and let her think.

He didn't get the chance to hear her answer. Just then, there was a discrete tap on his shoulder. He turned with a snarl, ready to pummel the person who dared to interrupt his scene and saw Candy the check-in girl.

"I'm sorry, Master Brice," she whispered with her head down and hands shaking. "I never would have bothered you, but your phone is going off in your locker. You said that I was supposed to come get you no matter what if it ever did that and, well...it did."

Brice bit off a nasty curse and immediately regretted it when Candy took a hasty step back. "It's all right, Candy. You were right to come and get me. Thank you." With a deep breath, he tried to wrestle his libido into submission. "Look, I have to go—that will be important. Will you help Terryn get home when I leave?"

"Oh, yes, Master," she replied, eager to please. "I'd love to. I'll take extra special care." Brice smiled at her and gave her an affectionate kiss on the cheek, then turned back to Terryn, who was slowly coming back to her senses.

"Oh, little fireball," Brice said, looking his fill at her— stretched, naked and very well used. "I have to leave. Nothing short of murder could pull me away at a moment like this, so I have no choice. It's work. Nobody else would call me this late." As he spoke, he started unbuckling and checking her limbs just in case the restraints had hurt her. "A Dom should always see to aftercare. It's my job to make sure you are pampered and well-tended after offering so much of yourself and pleasing me so well." As soon as she was free, he took the thick robe Candy had thoughtfully snagged and slipped it on Terryn.

"I want to see you again very soon. I don't have the right to be making any demands, but I will make a request." He cupped her softly pointed chin in his palm and looked deep into her eyes. "I would ask that you not come here again without me. I would ask that you allow me to be your Dom, at least for now." He brushed a fiery lock of hair back from her check and gently rubbed her earlobe between two fingers. "I am not usually a possessive man but I find I don't like the thought of another Dom touching you." Then he smiled and leaned down to whisper, "At least not without me there to watch."

Terryn gasped and let out a little moan. He smiled and thought she just might be perfect for him, if that thought turned her on. "So, will you wait for me?"

At first she took so long to answer he thought she was going to decline—he didn't like to think about what that did to his insides—then she nodded.

"Good," he said, and kissed her full and deep. "That's real good. Candy will give you my number and make sure she gets yours to me. I have to go."

To Candy he said, "Take care of her and when you get a cab for her, make sure she gets in it." He winked at Terryn and went to his locker.

He was a homicide cop. If he got called in to work after-hours, that meant only one thing—someone was dead. His libido would have to wait. He quickly gathered his things, and his phone went off just as he was leaving. With a snarl and a curse, Brice answered as he headed for the door.

Chapter Five

Katie Jernigan was tiny. According to her driver's license she was only five-one. In death she looked a lot smaller. Her miniature figure was crumpled on its side in the fetal position. Her small arms were slashed to ribbons where they had curled over her head, fruitlessly trying to protect her face from the relentless hacking of a knife. Several of her fingers were severed and lying around her while what remained were hanging on by threads of tendons and muscle tissue. If he were to judge by her clothing, she'd been out on a date. She was wearing a slinky black dress, high heels and matching jewelry. However the date had started out, it hadn't ended well.

The streetlamp was a ghastly spotlight on her crumpled form in the deserted parking lot. Brice crouched down to look closely at her without disturbing the scene. The forensic guys were snapping away with their cameras and until they were sure they'd gotten every inch and every possible angle of the crime scene, nobody was touching anything.

"Poor baby," he murmured to her when he could see under her arms. "It didn't help, did it? Bastard still got your pretty face." Pity wrenched his stomach into a hard ball of fury when he saw the jagged slice that split her cheek clean in two. The slash had been so vicious that it'd cut through the gum as well, displacing several of her teeth. There was a sickening pattern to the multiple stab wounds spread over her. They were deep and wild and committed with a brutal abandon that he had become all too familiar with lately. He gazed over the damage with a sinking heart and recognized the signature of Amber's killer as if the prick had signed his fucking name.

The attack had been aimed at her head. Chunks of scalp and what had once been streaky blonde hair lay scattered among the blood puddles surrounding her. Her ear with its dangling black earring was resting about three inches too high on her head. His guess? It must've got caught on the knife and plunked back down as her killer had kept stabbing. Her arms and shoulder got the worst of it; the shoulder looked like the psycho had tried to hack it off completely. There were a couple stabs to the ribs and kidney area that looked to him like they were thrown in for good measure after the killing frenzy had passed. They weren't as deep or clustered together as the ones surrounding her head.

He'd have to wait for the official report to be sure, but he'd bet his ass she'd been alive long into this attack. Brice knew there wasn't a thing he could do about that. About the pain and terror she must've gone through. But he could damn well make sure that she was the last girl this fucker butchered. He looked back to her face, saw past the damage to the girl and he made a promise that that's just what he would do.

"Fuck," Kent knelt down next to Brice and saw all that he did. "You recognize her, right? I hate this job."

"No," Brice returned without looking up. "You love it as much as I do."

"Are you kidding?" Kent's voice dripped with disgust at the waste of such a young life. "Nobody could fucking love this."

"No. Not this. But we're gonna love putting this fucker in a cage."

It was past dawn when Brice and Kent called time out and headed for their homes again. They had done all they could and needed down time and some sleep before they could take the next step. The precinct would send grievance counselors to inform her parents since they were out of state, so that was one duty off their shoulders. Meanwhile they would be tracing all of Katie's steps backward for the last days leading to her death. It was routine. Standard procedure. The thing was, nine times out of ten, standard procedures led them to the killer. No murder was perfect. There were always clues, and if he and his partner were good enough they would get the bastard and end this now.

Six hours later, Brice and Kent found themselves at the Surf-N-Slurp. "What a small world," Kent quipped. "Imagine, Amber and Katie working together. This could be just the break we need."

Brice smiled at the sweet woman at the counter. She had a fairly vacant look on her face, almost as though she wasn't quite sure what was going on around her and was more than a little surprised to find herself here. She was just shy of thirty years old and had a strong, solid build, not the wiry model-thin look that so many New York women had. Her blonde hair was thick and shiny. In Brice's opinion it was her best feature—it framed her pleasant face nicely and went well with her light blue eyes.

"Hello, officers," she greeted when she saw them, not quite making eye contact. "Welcome back. Can I get you something? Or are you here with news?"

"Hi, Mandy." He shook his head when she lifted a tray of muffins for him and Kent. "No sweets for me, thanks. I'll take a large drip coffee, no sugar, easy on the cream. Kent?"

"I'll have a double tall monkey madness with an extra shot of hazelnut." Kent said around a mouth full of the muffin.

Brice shook his head in awe. "Seriously? Dude? You're a cop. Where's your dignity, man?"

"Hey, back off my monkey madness," Kent said with all the dignity he had at his disposal considering that his cheeks were packed with double chocolate muffin and his coffee of choice was named after a zoo animal.

"You eat like an eight-year-old." Brice thought back and couldn't remember ever having a stomach that could take that much sugar in one sitting, even when he had been eight.

"Well, my diet keeps me young." Kent struggled to choke down a lump of gooey chocolate as he debated with Brice.

"Wrong," Brice shot back. "Your diet will put you in an early grave and in the meantime it just makes you immature. Which is a far cry from young, my friend."

Kent ignored the taunt, having heard it a million times by now, and gulped down his first hot swallow of chocolaty, nutty, banana coffee goodness with undisguised relish.

With coffee in hand, Brice asked Mandy, "Is there another girl on with you today? Maybe someone who can watch the counter for a minute so we can talk?"

"Ummm." Mandy acted as though she didn't quite understand the question and looked around the café as if the answer might be written on one of the walls. "Ummm. I'm not sure, Angie is working, but Katie is off and Amber is gone now and Jenny isn't here and I don't know."

Before she could keep going, Brice placed his hand over hers and asked, "Where's Angie?"

"Behind you, officers," Angie said as she came up to them. "Wassup? Any news yet?"

Brice turned and smiled at her. He'd only met her once when he'd interviewed all the employees after Amber's death, but he'd liked her. She was a straightforward, no-nonsense kind of girl. She'd cried quietly through the interview, answered all his questions directly and to the point. Even when her heart was so clearly broken and he could tell that she'd wanted to fall apart she hadn't; she'd just held it together and the only sign that she'd been devastated were the tears steadily and quietly dripping from her eyes.

Before he could ask her for a minute, she caught on that something was wrong. She had lovely Filipina features thanks to her mother and her almond-shaped eyes narrowed on him as the cautious cheer faded from her expression.

"What is it?" she demanded with a raised eyebrow and a hand on her hip. "What? I am not up to any more bad news. Let's just say that right now." *All New York sass and bravado,* Brice thought as she tried to ward off what she knew was coming. "'Cause I'm done with that, okay? I mean it. I don't care. I am not crying again and all that so just go on if that's why you came, 'cause really? Really? I'm done already and y'all haven't even talked yet so—yeah."

Brice could see the panic starting to build up as he and Kent continued to look at her. There was nothing they could do but watch as she slowly backed away from them and stumbled into a table.

"C'mon, sweetheart." Kent reached out and helped her to a chair. "Sit down and brace yourself for a minute." He looked into her eyes and would've given anything he owned not to do this to her. "This is gonna be bad. Brice? Do you want to lock the door?"

Brice headed for the front as Kent reached out and tucked her black hair behind her ear. It was thick as a horse's mane yet soft as silk, and Kent had been secretly wondering about how it would feel since they'd first met. She was alluring and sassy and he'd been coming in for coffee just for a glimpse of her whenever the case had let him come up for air.

She had black-framed glasses that slid on her face because her nose was too small. He thought it was sexy as hell whenever she peeked at him over them, and the way she splayed her fingers wide and used her palms to slide them back in place stirred him up just as much. Right now they were down again, so he just took them off completely, folded them and placed them in her lap. He'd been watching her these past days and knew she didn't need them to see close up.

"It's Katie, sweetie." Kent took a deep breath and finished quick, like ripping off a Band-Aid. "She's gone. We think it was the same guy who got Amber."

With a keening cry, she folded. Less than a week ago she lost one friend and coworker and now here they were again. Her thin arms clutched around Kent's neck and her face burrowed into his shoulder. The heartrending sobs shook her small frame from head to toe, so Kent scooped her up, sat in her chair and just let her cry it out. Stroking her hair and not saying a word as he rocked her and tried to offer what comfort he could. Nothing would bring her friend back, nothing would make it better, so all he had was this—he could hold her while she cried.

Brice watched with a dawning sadness. He hadn't known until this moment that Kent had felt anything for Angie. He'd known that Kent had thought she was hot—hell, who wouldn't? She was beautiful and though slender, she had curves in all the right places. But it was her smart mouth and keen wit that had probably done Kent in. His partner was a sucker for a girl with a sense of humor and a sharp tongue. He just hoped that the two of them could find a way to make this work when the dust settled.

"What? What is it? Is it Amber still?" Mandy asked, peering around Brice's shoulder to see. "I know it was so sad. We are all so sad. I didn't work with her long. Not like Angie, but I knew her and it was just so sad." Mandy shook her head and pursed her lips as she watched Kent and Angie.

Brice didn't know how she managed not to hear them tell Angie when she'd been standing right there, but figured it was up to him to fill her in. "Mandy, it's Katie. We think the same person got her that killed Amber."

"What?" She gasped, shock leached all the color from her already pale face, "Oh no! Oh no! It can't be! I knew her too! Not Katie! She was so sweet!"

And then she launched herself at Brice. He felt like he'd just been hit by a linebacker as she latched on to him with surprising strength. Her shrill wail blasted right into his ear. Unlike the delicate shudders that had run through Angie's body in her grief, Mandy's first jerking sob knocked him off balance since he wasn't expecting it, and they almost toppled onto the floor.

Oh hell no, he thought. "Mandy." If his voice was too sharp for the situation, it couldn't be helped. Sweet, vacant Mandy was squeezing hard enough to crack a rib and wailing loud enough to bust his ear drum "Mandy, stop. I need you to focus. We have to ask some questions and I need you to talk to me. Can you do that for me? Can you focus for just a moment? For Katie?"

"M-kay." With a wet slurping sound that could never be considered a sniffle, Mandy released her death grip on him and stepped back. "For Katie I will."

"When was the last time you saw her?" he asked in a more gentle tone now that he could breathe again. He took out his notebook and a pen.

"I saw her yesterday. We worked together all day. Then she went home and had a date. But I didn't see her after that. I didn't see her date, only her alone at work." She blinked at him, looking as confused as if she'd been asked what the square root of pi was. "And then she went home. For a date. But I didn't see her after that. After her date, I mean. Just here at work."

"Oh Lord." Angie gathered herself together and pushed up from Kent's lap to face Brice. "She left here 'bout six yesterday. Took the subway across the street just like normal. Katie rides the A train. She did have a date with one of our regulars. His name's Brian Gwin. They were supposed to have dinner and go dancing if it went well." She seemed to pull herself together as she spoke and by the time she looked past him to Mandy, her expression was kind. "Mandy? Can you go in the back and check on the muffins? They're gonna burn if we don't get them out. Don't forget to turn the oven off."

Mandy hurried to the back, and all three breathed a sigh of relief once she was out of sight. "I just don't get it," Angie said. "She seems normal when you look at her. She can do everything that you or I can, but something just is a little off, ya know? She's got just a little Forrest Gump thrown in there. Maybe they're related."

She shook her head with a rueful smile and Kent unsuccessfully tried not to laugh. "Forrest Gump?" he asked.

"Yeah," She looked up at him with a glimmer of her normal self coming to the surface. "You know, the Tom Hanks flick?"

Kent full out laughed at that and Brice knew then they were a match made in heaven.

After jotting down some more notes on Katie's last day of work, the two headed off to find Brian Gwin and see just how his date went last night.

Chapter Six

Brian was easy to track down. His had been the last call made from Katie's phone and he answered on the first ring when Brice called.

"Hello?" He had a deep voice that sounded like he might have still been asleep when he answered.

"Hello, Brian?" Brice replied. "This is Detective Brice Marshall and I need about five minutes of your time. Can you give me your whereabouts?"

"Huh?" The voice sounded a little clearer and a not a little confused. "Um, who is this?"

"Detective Marshall. Where are you right now?" His voice got firmer. "There is an urgent matter that we need to discuss."

"Oh, 'kay. Sure, I'm still at home, I got the day off so I was sleepin' in." He rattled off the address and Brice assured him they'd be there in ten minutes.

The young man who opened the door was six foot, blond, had blue eyes and good, strong features. He had a decent build, not muscled or ripped, but it was easy to see why Katie had gone out with him. Brice noted that he hadn't bothered to shower while waiting for them—it looked as though he had instead just gone back to sleep. He stood there at the door wearing worn-thin boxers, messy hair and a day's worth of stubble.

"Hi, Brian," Brice said. "Mind if we sit down?"

"Oh, sure," Brian stepped aside and gestured to the living room. It was spacious and surprisingly neat for a single guy. The carpet even had the lines that showed a recent vacuuming and there wasn't a dust bunny or empty cup in sight.

"Nice place you got here," Kent commented. "Who's your maid service?" As Kent and Brice sat, Brian shuffled his feet and, if Brice didn't know any better, blushed.

"Nah, no service. I'm, um, kind of a neat freak." When the men just stared at him, he shrugged. "What? I don't like a mess. Big deal. I like it clean, so I clean."

"Brian," Brice started, getting to the point because he wasn't sure Kent wouldn't get into a debate about the dangers of doing housework. His partner was a serious slob. "We understand that you had a date with Katie Jernigan last night?"

Bafflement marked his features and he said, "Yeah. So?" And his arms crossed over his chest. The defensive gesture was not lost on the detectives.

"Can you tell us how that went? What time the date ended?"

"It went great, why? We hit it off and stayed out for a while. I don't know what time I got home."

"So you went home alone?" Kent left a smirk in place to needle him; Brice knew he did it just to see if they could shake something loose.

"Yeah, alone." Brian's stance got even more defensive, his fists clenched where they were tucked under his pits and he braced his legs as though for a fight. "I mean, we fooled around a little. Just, it was our first date and we weren't ready to spend the whole night together."

"So? What?" Kent returned. "You bent her over in a dark alley and then said see ya?"

"Hey!" Brian's face flushed an ugly red and he took an aggressive step forward. "Watch it! You got no right to come in here and talk that way. And watch where you're going with that. She's a nice girl and even though it was our first date we've known each other a long time. And it wasn't in a freakin' alley, either. We, umm." He lost some of his steam and seemed to think twice about giving out the details. "Wait. What's this about? What happened? Is she in trouble for something?" He looked from one to the other of them. "Am I?"

"You're not in trouble." *Not yet, anyway,* Brice thought. "We need you to finish telling us about your date, though. Go on."

More cautious now, Brian continued, "We came back here. We weren't ready for an all-nighter, so I took her home after." He looked like he knew he was caught in a trap but didn't know what he could do about it.

"What time did you take her home?"

"I told you, I don't know. I wasn't keeping track."

"All right," Kent soothed, switching tactics to keep him off balance. "So you saw her safely home? You took her there yourself?"

"No. I'm a jerk-off who bags 'em and leaves 'em." Brian shot Kent a look that should've fried him on the spot. "'Course I saw her home. We left and took a cab to her place. I left her in front of the back door to her building 'cause she didn't want the neighbors asking questions if anyone saw me going up to her apartment. We kissed good night and I'm supposed to have dinner with her after her shift."

"Wait?" Brice zeroed in on that—he knew it was supposed to be her off day. "She's working today?"

"Yeah." Brian shrugged. "At her second job. She doesn't make enough at the Surf-N-Slurp so she took a part-time deal at that new rec center for girls, the Pink Ladies or something."

"Well, fuck me," Brice said under his breath as the rug was pulled out from under his feet.

"Yeah, me too," Kent agreed. "Small world."

"Why?" Brian asked, looking at their identical expressions of shock.

"Nothing," Brice answered. "It's just that my cousin and his family own that rec center." *And this is going to kill them.* He wondered fleetingly if Katie was the girl Riley had hinted at setting him up with. He hoped not. Riley had said the two of them were close and he didn't think he could stand breaking her heart that way.

"No kidding?" Brian shrugged again. "It *is* a small world. So, you guys wanna tell me why my love life is so interesting to a couple of cops?"

Brice looked at the guy, possibly the last person to see Katie alive, and braced himself for what came next. "Brian, Katie was found dead around two o'clock this morning in the parking lot behind her building. She was murdered. We need you to tell us everything you remember about last night. Every detail, no matter how small. I also need you to tell me how you got back home and if you saw or talked to anyone after you left her."

Back in the car outside Brian's building, Kent scrubbed at his face as though he could wash the fatigue away. "That was brutal. I didn't expect him to cry like that. What a mess."

"Yeah, who'da thought after one date he'd fall apart?"

"He did say they'd known each other a while."

"True, and didn't Angie say he was a regular?" Brice gave himself a mental pat for being subtle in bringing Angie's name up, nice and smooth.

"Fuck you," Kent said without making eye contact. "I ain't goin' there, so drop it right now." So much for subtle.

"Hey, I haven't said a word." Brice held up his hands in the classic surrender gesture.

"And let's keep it that way. I'm not ready to talk about it and I'll let you know when I am. Just drive."

Brice chuckled, glad he could find some humor in this dreary situation and headed for the Pink Ladies rec center for girls.

Terryn Keller was ticked off and exhausted. This was her seventh straight day at the rec center and her fourth double, since she'd have to work both the morning and evening shifts today. She'd been called in this morning to cover for Katie, who was a no-show. Terryn swore when she got her hands on that skinny little pixie she was going to squish her like a bug.

But as she thought it, she knew she wouldn't say a word. She loved Katie; she just couldn't believe that she'd gone and no-showed them like this. Katie knew that someone would have covered for her—all she had to do was ask. Well, Terryn sure hoped her date was worth it, because Trevor was spittin' mad about this and even though Terryn wished otherwise, she was afraid that this might just cost Katie her job.

Sure, Brian was cute and Terryn knew that Katie had been looking forward to their date all week. The two of them had hit it off like magic and Terryn hadn't blamed Katie at all for wanting to be alone with him. What she did blame her for, though, was leaving her holding the bag. Terryn had been wallowing in afterglow all morning and just when she was about to indulge herself in a nice long bubble bath for more glowing, she'd been called into work.

To make matters worse, Terryn was fed up with the place right now. She loved these girls, she loved the work and she even loved her bosses. She'd just been living and breathing all things tween for too long without a break. If she had to break up one more argument over who was hotter, Robert Pattinson or Taylor Lautner, she just might strangle herself with the nearest Miley Cyrus T-shirt.

She bent over the spa chair, tuned out the music and screechy chatter that only teen girls seemed capable of making and tried to focus on the motor and only the motor. If she could get the darn thing working before Trevor came in tomorrow, she'd know that there was a God and He liked her. The center was run one-hundred percent on donations and if she could save them the cost of a repairman it would mean that money could go for more important things. Besides, she liked working on stuff like this; she'd always had a knack for gadgets and motors. One of her favorite ways to burn off stress or relieve a little pent-up frustration was tinkering and today she had stress and frustration in spades. Just as that thought drifted through her mind, a gasket blew and water blasted her right in the face.

"Jiminy Crickets!" she yelled, fighting to get it secured before the room flooded. "Son of a biscuit-eatin' dog licker!"

Brice and Kent stopped dead in their tracks. They were two seasoned New York cops and yet her choice of cursing left them both dumbstruck. As her G-rated tirade continued to fly while she fought with a chair, the men struggled to maintain straight faces. Words like *scum-sucking* and *toot sniffer* floated around her and completely enchanted them both.

"Excuse me, miss?" Brice interrupted. "Can we have a word?"

She froze with comic suddenness and Brice could all but see the steam of embarrassment pouring up from her as she discovered she had an audience. Then every part of her wilted over the chair and she flopped her hands on the floor in defeat.

"Figures," she grumbled and pushed herself up to face them. "Of course there'd be someone standing there. Of course. I shouldn't even be surprised."

Then she turned around and Brice forgot his own name.

It was her. His redhead from last night. She was clothed in worn jeans and a ratty hoodie. She was flustered, wet and exasperated, and Brice felt every moment of their time together come to life in his body. In less than a second, he was hard and aching to pick up where they had left off, the case momentarily forgotten.

Terryn felt like she'd just been hit in the head. By lightning.

It was him. It was her Dom from last night. She cringed inwardly at what she must look like. It was just her luck that the sexiest guy in the universe would find her on a day when she was looking and feeling about as appealing as a sumo wrestler's toe jam. She felt a flutter of excitement that he had gone to the trouble to find her so soon, although it was tempered with apprehension. He was with another man and the two of them looked awful serious for a social call.

He gave her one of his smiles and said, "Hello, Terryn. This is my partner, Detective Brandon Kent. I take it you work here?"

Terryn rubbed her hands on her thighs and smiled at them. Wow, he was a cop. A detective, even. She tried not to let the cop fantasy that immediately sprang to life in her brain show on her face and said, "Guys, I feel like I live here. What can I help you with? Please tell me you're here because the NYPD wants to make a generous donation of their time and money."

"We wish." Brice didn't return her smile. Now that she'd pulled herself together after the surprise wore off, she could see he wanted to get this done. It made sense to her. If he was coming with bad news, she wouldn't thank him for spending ten minutes flirting with her before springing it. "Is Trevor or Riley around?" he asked.

Terryn shrugged. "No. Not today. I'm next in the chain of command if you're looking for someone in charge."

"Who's on with you right now?" They were in the salon room, which was empty and relatively quiet, but the game room and lobby they had passed to find her had been full to busting with squealing, giggling girls.

"I've got a couple of volunteers out in the main room somewhere, but I'm the only paid employee right now. We're short today, one called in sick and my friend from last night no-showed on us." She gave him a smile and an eye roll. "Guess they really hit it off, huh?"

"Is this a good place to talk?" Kent asked. He was looking at Brice with a frown and Terryn guessed that Brice hadn't told him about her. Since he had seemed just as surprised to see her as she had been to see him, she could understand why.

"Sure," she answered, "as good as any. Girls could come in any minute no matter where you go here. There is no hiding." This time her smile was a little forced as she caught on that this might not be a pleasant conversation. Dread turned her stomach into a cold hard ball and Terryn quickly started doing a mental roll call of all the girls who had come to the center this morning, trying to remember if one was missing.

"Terryn, your no-show, your friend, that's Katie Jernigan, right?"

"Yes."

"Katie was killed last night." As Terryn's eyes filled with tears and her bottom lip quivered, Brice looked as though he wanted to reach out to her, but then he fisted his hands instead and kept them at his sides.

"I'm sorry. What?" Her voice was strangled from the effort it took to hold back the tears but they fell anyway. "What? You don't mean our Katie? Not Katie Jernigan. What does your Katie look like? You must have them mixed up. Katie's a very popular name." Her lip continued to quiver and her hands clutched around her middle while she looked to them with the hope that they were indeed mistaken.

"I'm sorry, Terryn," Brice told her. "There's no mistake. It's her."

She stumbled back into the spa chair, her knees came up and her arms clutched around her legs as she buried her face in them and let the grief take her. Her small shoulders shook while she rocked and cried quietly.

"I'm sorry," she mumbled after a moment.

"Sorry? What are you sorry for?" Brice asked.

"You said you ha...ha...have questions," she managed to get out.

"It's all right," Detective Kent answered in a soft voice. "You take a couple minutes. Don't worry about us."

Terryn had known Katie for years. They'd become close pretty quickly and had spent a lot of time together both on and off work. She had a million memories of her, but all she could think about right now was that she'd been angry at her for not showing up today. Katie had been lying somewhere dead and Terryn had been thinking about squishing her. Guilt, regret and sorrow made a cocktail of misery in her chest that she knew she'd never shake.

She slowly became aware that one of the detectives wanted her attention. Her couple minutes must be up, she thought. She could feel him at her side, crouched down next to her. After a sniffle and a deep breath, she turned her head to face Brice and his questions.

"We need to ask you our questions and then we need to get someone in here so you can go home," Brice said softly.

Terryn thought he had the voice of an angel. It was deep and soft and had such a rich tone to it that she wished he'd just keep talking so she could focus on that instead of the fact that her friend was dead.

Brice had to clench his fists in order to keep from reaching out to her. Her wild hair was a copper blaze around her face and grief had made her emerald eyes sparkle like polished jewels. Her freckled nose was red from crying and if she didn't stop that bottom lip from its quivering he didn't think he'd be able to resist scooping her up and cuddling her the way Kent had held Angie.

It was disconcerting to him. He'd never been in a position where work overlapped his personal life like this. He'd looked into things for family members before, but work had never involved a woman he was seeing. She looked adorable and heartbreaking right now and every dominant male gene he possessed was clamoring for him to carry her off somewhere where she'd never hurt again.

"I don't need to go home. I don't want to. There's no one there and nothing to do, so I'd rather just stay here and keep busy."

"We'll see how you feel when we're done. I'm going to call Trevor and Riley, get them in here."

"Oh, do you have to?" Terryn asked. "They have been working so hard lately—it's the first weekend they've taken in a month."

Brice knew they worked hard at both this girls' center and the one down the street for boys, but this wasn't something that could be delayed. He looked at Kent with a raised eyebrow. Kent shrugged, letting Brice know it was up to him.

"Terryn," Brice looked back to her. "If we don't get them in here, there has to be someone we can. If you don't want to leave, that's fine, but you are going to need some help dealing with this."

With a shuddering breath, Terryn gave in and fished her cell out of her pocket. As she dialed she told them, "I'll call Barb, I guess. She's the other manager here and she wouldn't mind coming in."

"Terryn, I know this is hard, but I need to know everything about last night up until we met," Brice said as soon as Terryn hung up her cell phone.

Terryn looked at him with horror leeching all the remaining color from her face. "Am I a suspect?"

"No, Terryn, no," Brice rushed to reassure her. "The M.E.'s already confirmed time of death and since that time was when we were together, I think you've got a pretty solid alibi." He saw her process that and then she seemed to take herself in hand with a deep breath and began.

"Well, we met at her apartment so we could get ready together." Her voice was so thin and quivery that it was broke his heart.

"What time was that?"

Terryn answered him quietly and clearly. Then she took them through each step of the night the same way. She answered every question without wanting to know why they asked and never batted an eye when she had to repeat herself. Brice lost count of the number of times she pulled herself back from the brink of hysterics. She handled the whole ugly questioning without losing it, though, and Brice felt inordinately proud of her for it.

After every possible angle of the night had been exhausted, Brice said, "I think we have enough for now. I'll have more questions for you later. For now, let's just see if that other manager is here."

By that time the sweet, motherly Barb had come in and had taken over. Barb's hazel eyes were puffy from crying, but other than that she held it together and was in control. In a matter of minutes, she had Terryn ensconced in the theater room with a small group of girls and enough junk food to make them all sick.

"She'll be best in there," Barb said. "Movies are her drug of choice and I picked a good tearjerker for them. They'll all lose themselves in the movie and cry together. Also, the girls I sent in there are some of her favorites. They'll bolster each other and keep their hands and minds busy in the meantime."

On the way to the door, she patted and stroked girls as they passed, reaching out with the loving strokes of a mother that so many children lacked at home. Brice noticed how each and every one she touched responded to the petting like well-fed kittens and thought that Barb was well suited to this work.

"Be sure and tell Trevor and Riley I'll be here all day today and tomorrow." Her voice was as soothing as her touch when she said to them, "As long as they need, I'll be here. You tell them I'll take care of everything and not to worry. I'll be praying for those sweet girls and their families." She shook her head sadly and closed the door behind them on her way back to Terryn and the children.

Brice took comfort in his surety that he was leaving them all in the best possible care. Then he steeled himself for what had to come next, telling Riley and Trevor that one of their own was dead.

One a.m. was not the ideal time to shop for groceries. Unfortunately, Brice had let work take over his life so completely that he'd even run out of toiletries, so he was out of options. He knew he had to compartmentalize, if he let every case consume him he'd be burned out before he hit forty. Knowing that, however, did not make this particular case release its death grip from his throat. As he loaded items into his cart from the toiletry aisle and rounded the corner to the medicine section, he tried to force thoughts of the case to their proper compartment, and there was Terryn.

Suddenly the case went away and his mind was his own again. He smiled as he realized it. *Leave it to a Marshall,* he thought, *all we need is a beautiful woman and everything's right in our world.*

She was dressed in those clingy workout pants that women wear to yoga class and a tank top. He watched as she tucked her hair behind her ear while she read the labels in front of her and worried her thumbnail between her teeth. She wasn't biting it, but he could tell that it was a close call. If the stress didn't let up, he'd give her perfectly groomed nails two days, tops. She tilted her head to the side and closed her eyes. He could see the misery and tension on her as clear as day.

"Hey, Red," he said. "How're you holding up?"

She startled a little and gave him big eyes when she turned to him. He could tell when recognition set in by the way her shoulders relaxed.

"Hi, Brice...um, detective." Her smile was slight and didn't come close to quenching the misery in her emerald eyes. "Not well, I'm afraid." She motioned to the items in front of her. "Can't sleep, and yoga didn't help, so..."

Brice looked at the choices of over-the counter sleep aids and reached out to rub a hand over her shoulder. He meant to keep it brief, but Terryn laid the side of her face on his hand before he pulled away. The soft skin felt like satin to him and he turned his palm until he cradled her cheek. Her eyes closed and a tear slipped out of the corner of one to trickle onto him. He stepped around the cart to bring her into his arms with a shushing murmur when she tensed, and then settled her against his chest.

With a sob, Terryn wrapped her arms around Brice and clung. It'd been two days since she found out about Katie. For two days she'd been alone with her grief. Nothing made it go away, nothing made it hurt less. She had tried eating, only to find it impossible to get food past her lips without gagging. She tried to just let herself cry, thinking it would empty her out and leave her blessedly numb, but the tears never stopped and it didn't help the pain. It was relentless. Yoga and jogging were equally useless and even the ancient exercise video she tried had failed.

"Nothing helps. Nothing makes it better." It wasn't until his arms tightened around her and he murmured a "Shhh" in her ear that she realized she'd said the last thought out loud.

She heard him whisper, "C'mere." Then he was leading her toward the café area, his cart forgotten. He guided her into a booth and sat next to her. Without reasoning the how or why of it, she just accepted the comfort he offered and snuggled into his side with a hiccupping sigh.

"I moved here from Nevada right after college." She didn't know why the words came pouring out of her, they just did. "We lived there my whole life. Not too far from Las Vegas. My parents still live there. It's a small, dusty town with nothing to do and nothing to look at but sagebrush. I wanted out of there so bad." Someone had left an empty water bottle on the table, so Terryn reached out and fiddled with the label as she spoke.

"I was sick of the desert and sick of small-town living. I wanted adventure and skyscrapers and a big city life that my mom could brag about to her friends. I thought I was prepared for this. I thought New York would be such an exciting and great place to live." It was easy to look back now at how frightened and dismayed she'd been. She shook her head and told him, "I was scared out of my mind. How can such a small city be so big? It's crowded and grimy and people are everywhere."

Terryn snuggled closer and wrapped her arms around him again. "Katie was the first real friend I made here. We met at the Surf-N-Slurp. I was going to go back home that weekend and then Katie was so sweet to me. She made eye contact and when she asked me how I was doing, I thought she actually wanted to know." When Terryn smiled at the memory, she realized that it was the first time she'd smiled in two days. "Funny. We hadn't even really made friends yet, but that night I cancelled my moving truck. Katie showed me that there was hope. New York wasn't all bad." Tears started steadily trickling down her cheeks again and Terryn said, "Now New York killed her."

Brice clutched her tighter in his arms. "Aw, baby," he said. "Not New York. New York didn't kill her. Just one twisted asshole. I'm gonna find that asshole and put him in a cage."

Terryn tightened her arms around him again and whispered, "Promise?"

"Promise," he whispered back, and Terryn was sure she felt his muscles quake with his vehemence.

Chapter Seven

I can't believe how brainless they all are! She was just another slut! Putting out on the first date? Why aren't I getting a medal for this? She was pathetic and stupid. All she did was curl up and scream like a baby. "Ooohh! How could you do this? Oooooh! Please stop!" Ooooh, what a bitch. She wasn't near as good as Amber. Maybe next time I'll try a baseball bat. That should be fun.

Terryn got ready for the funeral all alone in her basement apartment. As she dressed, it was with the careful slowness of a woman much older than her own twenty-six years. Each movement and action was chosen with an almost ritual concentration that she somehow felt reflected how much Katie had meant to her.

Terryn hadn't made a lot of friends in this city. Most were coworkers and of them Katie had been her closest. She was too focused on her work and a little shy, so making friends had never been easy for her. Katie was the only one who could ever get her out of her shell. It was her influence and support that got Terryn to explore outside her comfort zone. With a no-nonsense approach, she took the lead on the whole BDSM mystery, and without her Terryn would never have had the guts to try. Katie had always pushed Terryn to let herself go and let her inner wild child play.

She looked in the mirror and could almost hear what Katie would've said: "C'mon, Terryn. You've gotta sex it up if you don't want to spend all your nights with a battery-operated boyfriend. Black is so not your color—why don't you wear that bronze dress we bought in SoHo? It looks fab on you and you know it."

The phantom Katie she visualized was dancing around the room like the real Katie had always done in life, never still for a minute. Her boundless energy propelling her from one spot to the next like one of the ballerina figurines in a jewelry box, head high, arms raised, and she never stopped twirling. With perfect clarity, Terryn could see Katie march right up behind her, put her fists on her hips and challenge, "Let your hair down, for crying out loud. And put on some makeup. What are you doing? Going to a funeral?"

With a hiccupping cry, Terryn ripped the black, shapeless dress from her body and flung it across the room. She then yanked out the clips holding her bun in place and threw them with enough force that one broke when it hit the wall. With visions of Katie's laugh and her challenging remarks still whirling through her mind, she grabbed the dress Katie had picked out for her from the back of the closet. It was clingy and sexy and completely inappropriate for a funeral, but she didn't care.

This was for Katie and she would do her proud.

Brice got to the funeral late. The mourners were filing by the front slowly to give their condolences to the family. It wouldn't give him a lot of time to observe everyone but he'd hang back and see what he could. He always came to the funerals if the killer was still at large. The way people acted gave him insights that led in some very fruitful directions. He was scanning the crowd of somber and weeping mourners when he caught sight of Terryn. She stopped his breath.

Standing at the back of the room, she was dressed in killer heels with spikes that had to be five inches at least. Her long and shapely legs were displayed to mouthwatering perfection in a dress that was sin in material form. It was the color of the desert at sunset and it presented her body like a gift. Every inch of her was outlined in silk. The endless lines of her legs were bare up to mid-thigh, where the dress lovingly clung then embraced an ass that was so flawless in shape it made his palms sweat. That glorious auburn hair had been straightened and it glowed against her shoulders like polished copper. She would've stood out in the middle of a Hollywood red carpet, but in this setting she shone like beacon in the night.

"That's some dress, Red," he whispered from behind her.

She turned to him with a slight grimace and said, "I know. I had an aneurism or something." She gestured self-consciously. "I was in a nicely hideous black dress when I looked in the mirror and heard Katie." Tears filled and fell from her eyes, and a small smile curved her lips. "I swear I did. She was teasing me like she always did because I never dress up. Katie was always making me go shopping with her and pushing things like this dress on me. I've never had the guts to wear it, and she never stopped harassing me about it. So, for her...for her I wore it today."

Brice took the time to look his fill. She was lethal. Her straightened hair was held back with some clips so the exquisite symmetry of her features was evident. He let his gaze lower past her slender neck and almost-bare shoulders, where the dress was held on by delicate straps. Her waist flowed in an hourglass curve to a flat tummy and perfectly rounded hips. He

68

swallowed audibly when he saw that her legs looked just as tempting from the front as they did from the rear view, long, tan and slender.

He said the only thing he could think of: "You look like a walking fantasy."

She laughed softly. "Then I did her proud, I guess. Thank you."

"Can I help you to your seat?" he asked, hoping there would be an empty one next to it so he could stay close even though the service was all but over.

"No, it's almost done and I couldn't sit still any longer. Thanks, though." She smiled at him again. He was getting hooked on those smiles.

"Well, I'll stay here with you then and stand guard."

"Stand guard?" she asked, puzzled.

"In this dress? You need it, even if we are in a church."

The Surf-N-Slurp was closed to the public for the day in memory of Katie. After the service and reception, a small group of Katie's friends and co-workers gathered at the coffee shop. More to avoid going home and facing her lonely apartment, Terryn was one of them. The café was crowded with people who she could only assume felt the same. Terryn noticed that Kent wasn't straying far from Angie and wondered if the two of them had had an official date yet. She knew Angie pretty well and didn't think the poor girl even realized that she was in love with him.

Terryn saw Brice head her way out of the corner of her eye and sat up a little straighter in her chair. There was just something so captivating about the man that made her sit up and pay attention. She knew that it was cliché to hook up at a time like this; people needed to reaffirm that they were alive and to find that most basic of comfort. Cliché or not, she might just see if the yummy Detective Marshall could be persuaded to take her home. He'd been kind and polite to her since he'd come to the center and told her about Katie. Right now she would give just about anything to get him to drop the detective persona and bring out the Dom she remembered from that first night. She had a suspicion that if he'd tie her up again, he could make her forget everything.

"How are you holding up?" Brice asked, taking a seat next to her. He was dressed in a black silk shirt and slacks that fit him so well they had to be tailor-made.

"Um, I'm fine." She shrugged one shoulder and tucked a stray lock of hair behind her ear. "Well, not really. I want to say something about how I feel. But everything that comes to mind sounds shallow and stupid. No wonder everybody always says the same things when they lose someone—it's all there is to say." She looked into his eyes and asked him, "Do you want to know what I've discovered over the last three days? There are a total of five acceptable phrases."

"Five?" he asked, reaching out to brush his fingers along her brow.

"Five," she replied, tilting into his touch as chills raced up and down her arms. "Five sentences sum it all up. 'I can't believe she's gone. She was so young. She had so much life left to live. I still can't believe it'." Her voice broke and she reached up to press his hand until he was cradling the side of her face when she said the last one. "I don't know how I'm going to live without her."

A tear trembled and fell from the corner of her lashes and she saw Brice watch it slide over her cheek to pool at the edge of her lips. He said, "Ah, Red," then took her by the hand and helped her to her feet. "C'mere." Without letting go of her hand, he walked into the hall leading to the restrooms. Terryn thought he was bringing her there so she could wash her face but when she reached out to open the door of the women's room Brice gently turned her until she was backed into the wall and dipped his head.

At the first touch of his lips, Terryn felt all her muscles clench as she held her breath. The kiss was tender and sweet. His mouth gently nuzzled hers and when she didn't draw away or stop him, his tongue came out light as a feather and traced along her bottom lip until she opened for him. Then gentleness gave way to more. His mouth sealed over hers with a quiet groan and his tongue delved inside to stake his claim. The tender hand on her cheek slid to the back of her neck and gripped a fistful of hair; he used it to tilt her for a better angle and turned up the heat. Terryn's breath caught on a small moan at the mastery of the move.

She broke away with a gasp. "Wow." And when he used his mouth on the skin just below her ear, "Oh really, wow."

"I want you to get your coat and meet me outside. Right now." He looked into her eyes. She guessed he was judging to see if she was scared. She wasn't, but it was nice he wanted to make sure. "All right?"

"Yes." Terryn was a little nervous. After all, the club wasn't open this early, so that meant someplace private. However, she wanted this, she wanted him and she wanted to just feel something other than grief.

"Go ahead, I just have to say goodbye to my cousin and his family first."

Riley stood between her husbands and Brice saw that each of them had a hand on her, stroking in comfort.

"Hey, beautiful, wanna run away with me?" His heart eased to see her smile at his tired line. "We are going to find this guy, Riley. I promise."

As he clasped hands with her, he looked at first Trevor and then Cade, letting them know without words that he was hurting for them too. It turned out Katie *had* been the girl Riley had been hoping to set him up with and this was killing them all. She'd been a frequent guest of theirs these last months and was more than just Riley's friend.

"I know you will. You're my hero." Riley's face crumpled. "Now you'll be hers too."

"Ah hell, honey." Trevor's voice cracked as he said, "Don't cry again. Please, little one, I am going to break in two here."

Brice hated how this was hurting her. He hated how it was hurting them all.

"So," Cade said as he rubbed comforting circles on Riley's back, "Let's talk about something less painful for a moment. Terryn, hmm?" He gestured with his chin to where they could see her saying goodbye to the cafés owner, Jenny. "You sure about that?"

When Riley gasped, Brice quirked a brow and said, "I'm sure it's not any of your business, cuz."

Riley reached out and grabbed his wrist. "Oh, Brice. I know you just said it wasn't our business, but Terryn is not like us. I mean she has never been to our club or any club like it." When Brice's expression clued her in that she was stepping out of line, she hastened to explain. "I know she's beautiful. God, I wished I looked half as good as she does, but, honey, she's sweet." She leaned close and whispered, "Brice, she goes to church."

Brice chuckled and whispered back, "So do you." Before she could answer, he continued, "Riley, I love you like it's nobody's business, but this doesn't concern you."

He could have left it at that. In all probability, he should have, if Terryn hadn't confided to them that she was exploring the BDSM lifestyle herself. Brice couldn't, though. Riley was dear to him and already hurting, so he wasn't going to add worry on top of it all. "I met Terryn in the club, Riley. She's a new sub and I promise I'll take good care of her." His look chided as much as his words. "You should know me better than that."

Riley looked nonplused for a minute. Trevor looked at Cade and asked. "Why didn't you say anything?"

"I would have, eventually. As it stands, she's only just started. I wanted to give her the chance to settle in before I told her the club belonged to us." With a sigh and a sad shake of his head, he added, "In any event, I would've thought Katie had told her. Katie was the one who was showing her the ropes."

Riley looked back at Brice and took a deep breath. "You're right. I'm sorry. I'm just so out of it. But just be easy, 'kay? Our lifestyle is shocking to people who are new to it."

"You took to it like a cat to cream, Ry." Cade's whisper had the desired effect—Riley was distracted for a moment and blushed when she turned to look up at him. Brice shook each man's hand and laid a kiss on Riley's cheek before he turned and headed out to where Terryn waited for him on the sidewalk. It was time to put the grief and the case away for a while—he had a sub to claim.

Chapter Eight

Terryn stood on the sidewalk. It was a muggy day, the air warm and heavy. She closed her eyes and let the heat soak in as she waited. With her face tilted up to the sun and her mind on absorbing the warmth, she didn't hear Brice until he whispered in her ear, "You're incredible. Your hair looks like it's on fire in the sunlight." She stopped basking and smiled at him shyly, a little embarrassed that he'd caught her at it.

"Thank you." As he hailed a cab, she asked, "So, have you and Cade always been close?"

"Yes." A yellow cab pulled up. Brice helped her in and gave the address to the driver. "Cade's father and mine were the only two boys born to our grandparents and the two were thick as thieves. But that was nothing compared to how close and fast the mothers hooked up. We never went long without a visit growing up; we still don't."

"And are you and Cade the only boys too? Or are there more Marshall men out there?"

"There are more of us, and girls too. Both our fathers wanted big families and they got them." Brice's smile was disarming and warmed something deep inside her.

"How did you all meet Trevor?"

Brice sat close enough that his leg was pressed to hers and he slid one arm behind her shoulders. He used his free hand to play with the ends of her hair. "The Wellingtons are very close to the Marshall clan, especially to Cade's parents. Those two were practically raised together. If it weren't for their habit of sharing the same woman, I'd have said they were more brothers than friends."

Her face turned crimson and she stammered when she asked, "Is...are they? Um...how is it...um, do you know? Between them? Are they gay? Or...never mind. It's not my business, I shouldn't have asked." She hid her flaming cheeks against his shoulder with a groan of embarrassment.

Brice cupped a hand under her chin and urged her to meet his eyes. "They aren't gay, no. Though they have ample opportunity and no one that matters to them would care, they simply aren't inclined to go that way. They just enjoy sharing the same woman. They have since their college days. And when they met Riley, all bets were off. They knew she was the one for them right off the bat. I did too, the first time I saw them all together." She smiled at him, hearing the sincere affection in his voice.

The cabbie barked out the fare when the cab stopped. Brice paid and helped her from the car, his hand warm and steady in hers. Terryn felt butterflies explode to life in her stomach as she faced his building and what was to come.

"Whew." Terryn put a shaky hand on her fluttering tummy. "Can I tell you I'm nervous? Can I tell you I'm scared to take this step outside of the club?" She looked at him and the frown of concern on his breathtaking face. "Can I tell you that even with all that going on I still want this so bad I can taste it?"

Brice stepped closer to her until there wasn't a breath of space between them. He slid both of his hands into her hair and tugged her head back. At first his lips only rubbed against hers, lightly and then with more pressure. Terryn tried to open and take the kiss deeper, but Brice tugged hard on her hair and growled a command to hold still. The sound was primal. Terryn reacted to it instantly as every submissive gene in her body started to hum. Once she was still, he brought his mouth back to hers. He nibbled and sucked at her until her lips felt swollen and ultra-sensitive.

He broke the kiss to murmur, "Remember your safe word." He kissed a blazing trail to her ear. "Nothing that happens will be beyond your control." Then he took the tender lobe of her ear between his teeth and bit.

Terryn shot up to her toes. With a gasp, she clutched at his wrists while ricochets of sensations shot from that spot to echo in other more intimate areas.

Brice's whisper deepened when he said, "I know I asked at the club, but things have changed. I'm not asking anymore. You're mine. Now, I hope you don't have a problem with that because it won't make a damn bit of difference if you do."

His hot, wet tongue delved into the sensitive shell of her ear. Even though it wasn't a question, Terryn sensed that Brice was waiting for her compliance, so she nodded. It was all the agreement he needed because he said, "Done." Grabbed a hold of her wrist and marched them into his building.

"Whoa." She stumbled to a halt as soon as they stepped off the elevator into his penthouse. "Oh wow. Look at this apartment. This is beautiful."

Brice smiled at the awe in her voice. "You should see my cousin's place"

Terryn said, "It would be pretty hard to outshine this." Her head whipped from side to side as Brice continued to lead her through, trying to take it all in. It was gorgeous. Comfortable and homey rather than elegant, it was also bigger than almost any house she'd ever seen.

"Are you on the take?"

Nothing else could've stopped Brice at that moment. He had her in his apartment and he had her compliance. Desire that he'd been forced to regulate and ignore blazed to full intensity the second the doors had opened. The outrageous question did the impossible, though, and surprised a full-blown laugh out of him.

"I make decent money at the rec center," she was saying, "thanks to my awesome bosses, but wow, I couldn't come close to a place like this." She was teasing him, hands on her hips and a glint in her eye. Brice felt his laughter simmer back toward desire as she faced him so mischievously.

"I have a modest family income that allows me some things that my salary could not," he replied as he stalked over to where she stood. Slowly, purposefully, he circled her. When he saw she was about to say something else, he ran a single finger up the bare, tempting line of her spine. "We can talk more later. Starting right now you will only speak when given permission."

Her breath hitched and goose bumps bloomed along the trail he continued to make on her back and shoulders. "You will call me Sir until I release you to do otherwise." Brice stepped close and traced patterns across her delectable cleavage, then breathed the next words into the warm hollow below her ear.

"Now I want you to remove your clothes, clasp your hands behind your back and stand with your feet spread wide." Terryn did so with a honeyed whimper. Brice barely managed to keep his hands to himself as he watched. Her body was sleek and graceful. She moved fluidly and her pale skin seemed to glow in the light streaming in from the window.

Once she was naked and standing as ordered, Brice circled her again. "Nice. Very nice," he said in a low voice as he took in the sight of her bare ass. "Have you ever been taken here, sub?" He whispered in her ear to tempt her while he stroked between those lovely cheeks. She rewarded him with more goose bumps and gave a tiny shrug.

"Permission to speak?" she asked in a breathy voice. He took a suckling bite of her neck before he answered that she could. "I have only had men use their fingers there, and once a toy." Her answer brought a flush to her skin.

Interesting, Brice thought. "Did you enjoy that? The toy as well as the fingers?" The shaky nod she gave was not necessary since his finger was still gently running along the crease of her ass and her body was answering for him. A flush swept up her neck and heated her cheeks and when he slipped his hand farther between her legs he found that she was already wet. Terryn's knees almost buckled when he reached farther still to circle her clit and spread the moisture there before pulling away to stand in front of her.

"Terryn, keep your eyes on me." Slowly Brice unbuttoned his shirt and his own eyes blazed as he stared at her. "Bring your hands forward, Terryn, and show me where you want my mouth."

For a second she hesitated. He arched a brow and warned, "If I have to repeat myself, you won't like the consequences." Tentatively, her hands slid to brush her nipples. "Harder, Terryn. Pinch them harder for me. The way you want me to once I get my hands on them." He rewarded her with a hum of pleasure when her dainty fingers plucked with more force, turning the dusky pink tips a deep rose.

Once he got his shirt off, he backed up until he felt a chair behind him. He sat with deliberate slowness and removed his shoes and socks. Her breathing was erratic now and her lovely breasts were plumped nicely with the nipples teased into flawless, tight peaks.

"Come stand next to me." She staggered him when, instead of walking shyly or timidly, she strutted toward him as confident and seductive as a siren. She stopped in front of him with head bowed and waited for his next command.

It took him a moment to rein in the urge to drag her to the floor and pound out the raging lust she had inspired. With a tilt of his head, he motioned her closer between his spread legs. "You're glistening, Terryn." His eyes fixed on her core. "Touch your cunt for me." The fingers that slid to that alluring flesh trembled slightly and Brice bit back a moan. "Don't part the lips yet. Tease yourself first."

She hesitated for no longer than a second, then tickled her long fingers slowly along the crease where thigh met more tender flesh, just barely scraping her nails there. Next she made tiny circles up one tender labia, then did the same down the other. When she started petting the line where the two lips met, he ached with the need to replace her fingers with his tongue.

Brice loved watching a woman touch herself, it was a trigger that uncaged a beast within him. "Now put one foot on the arm of the chair so you can touch deeper."

Terryn made a noise in her throat that was a cross between a sob and a moan but did as she was ordered. With her foot on the chair arm and her other foot firmly planted on the floor between his knees, it put her open pussy right in front of his face. He could see every gloriously spread inch of her.

Her nails were painted a clear gloss with a sprinkle of gold glitter that shimmered as she rubbed them along the path his tongue wanted to take. They circled her plump clit, then stroked down to delve knuckle-deep inside, only to pull out and start all over again.

Brice thought he could detonate right then. When he sensed she was about to come, he clamped a firm hand on her wrist with a growl. With nostrils flared to catch the full bouquet of her scent, he brought her hand to his mouth as she watched him with wide, glassy eyes. Terryn was panting in erratic puffs. A cry escaped her once he caught her fingers between his lips. The taste exploded on his tongue and cut short the games he had intended to play.

"Enough." He motioned her back as he stood and then, with her wrist still clutched in his grip, headed for his room. "I need you in bed. Right fucking now."

On the other side of the city at a tiny little seafood grotto on the Hudson River, Brandon sat across the table from Angie.

"So." Angie looked at him with those melted chocolate eyes and said, "This is our first official date. What made you decide on today?"

Kent shrugged casually and said, "I hadn't planned it or anything. I just saw Brice grab hold of Terryn back at the coffee shop and then head out with her and I asked myself what the hell I was waiting for. So, I asked you if you'd eaten yet, you said no and here we are."

Angie smiled at him, reached out and brushed her fingers across the top of his where they rested on the table and said, "Yeah. Here we are. Terryn hadn't mentioned that she was dating Brice. We're not as close as her and Katie were, but we still go out sometimes. I'm surprised she didn't tell me." She shrugged. "Well, I'm just glad she's not alone right now." The look she gave him melted his heart. "I'm glad I'm not either."

It'd been a drive to get her here. But a nice one. She'd laid her head back against the seat and watched the Hudson as they'd wound their way toward it and after about five minutes in the car she'd taken his hand and held it all the rest of the way. The place was out of the city, hardly anyone ever around, and it was the best food he'd ever eaten. He wanted his first date with Angie to be a hit and Chuck's was the only place he could go that he knew would never let him down. Tucked right up against the water, it had a killer view of the river and this time of year the trees that were surrounding the place were alive with colors and the chirping of birds.

He felt like his whole world balanced on this date, and what the hell was he supposed to do with that? He took a steadying breath and told himself to chill.

"So," Angie interrupted his impending panic attack. "Is this a favorite place of yours?"

"Yeah. You won't find better or fresher fish than here at Chuck's," he answered with pride. "Guy used to own a fishing boat and do the Alaska to Seattle thing. He saved up, then sold his boat to buy this place here. The great thing is he has all his old fishing contacts so he gets his fish direct."

"Sounds great." Angie smiled at him. "You know this place, so why don't you order for me? Just don't be ordering me anything slimy or raw, 'cause then I'd have to throw up on you."

"Got it." He winked and waived the waitress over. Once the food came, fragrant and plentiful, the two dug in with gusto and Kent smiled as he watched her eat like a woman who wasn't afraid to show her appetite.

"What are you smiling at?" she asked, peeking at him over her glasses in that cute way that drove him nuts.

"You," he replied, his smile widening. "I'm glad you're here. I've been wanting to ask you out for a while, but with all the drama I didn't think it would be cool. I thought you needed some time first."

"Time? For what?"

"To grieve. I didn't want you thinking I wasn't sensitive to your needs." He felt a flush warm his cheeks when she snorted out a laugh.

Before he could come up with something appropriately masculine to restore his alpha male status, she reached out and touched his hand again. "That's sweet. But really? I've been waiting for you to ask me out since that first day. I was gonna start spitting in your coffee if you didn't do it soon. I swear I was. I ain't lying. You barely made it. I was even thinking I was going to have to go out and get myself arrested or something just to get you to notice me."

His eyes heated and he said, "Angie, I noticed you the second I set eyes on you."

Her cheeks bloomed with pleasure at that. She pulled her hand back and reached for the hot sauce. As she proceeded to drown her seafood sample platter in so much heat it made his mouth burn just to watch, she said, "By the way...no butt sex."

Kent inhaled instead of swallowed the shrimp in his mouth and as he coughed and choked, she continued without looking up, "I mean it. No butt sex. I don't get why anyone would do that, ya know?" She took a large bite of Atlantic cod, chewed a couple times and kept talking. "But everybody talks about it, so I tried it. Once. And I didn't like it. Yeah, ow. In a big way. And my friends were all like, you just gotta relax, and um, no. That's it. Just no. It hurts and it's gross and um, yeah...*no*. So don't even ask, 'cause that's a deal breaker with me. Let's just get it right out in the open there. You got plenty of other places you can put things, so that ride is closed. For good. Forever."

Kent was laughing out loud by the time she finished. He stood up to lean over the table and held her face between his hands. He kissed her softly and sweetly and melted the rest of her words into a sigh. "Okay. No butt sex. I promise." Then he sat back down and picked up his fork. "What did you mean by 'things', though? What 'things' did you want me putting in your 'other places'?"

Her deep brown eyes smiled at him, full of warmth, and Kent felt himself tumble happily into love when she winked and said, "We will just have to wait and see what you got up your sleeve." Then she popped a sauce-covered shrimp into her mouth. Kent tried not to drool as he watched her tongue come out and lick a dab of red from the corner of her lips.

"You know, I think I could get behind finding one of your places with one of my things right now." He looked up from her mouth and locked gazes with her. "How about you?"

She licked more sauce from her finger and said, "I can work with that. Pay the check."

Out in the parking lot, Kent had Angie plastered to the car and his hands adhered to her ass like they were glued to it. She panted as he worked one knee between her legs and applied pressure, then she mewled like a kitten when he tore his mouth from hers to kiss his way down her neck to the swell of her breasts.

"Fuck," he moaned, "Fuuuuck. You feel so good."

His hands squeezed harder on the cheeks of her ass and moved her on his thigh, grinding her just right so she'd shiver and moan again. "I can't wait to get inside you. I want you so fucking much."

When she quivered and clutched at his hair, he lost it and pulled her up. Fitting himself between her thighs, he ground against where she was melting-hot and wet. Her skirt was gathered up across her hips and her legs lifted and locked around his ass. It made him feel crazed that there was only one skimpy layer of panties and his zipper keeping him from being inside her.

He bit down on her nipple through the layers of dress and bra, then mumbled, "I can't put you down. I want you right here. Right now. You gotta stop me. I don't have it in me to stop myself." Then he tugged at both layers of material with his teeth until her dusky breast popped free. With a moan he latched on to the crest like a starving man at his last meal.

"Are you kidding me?" she half-panted, half-yelled. "You freaking stop and I'll punch you." Then she shimmied one hand between them and squeezed his shaft before tugging the zipper down.

Kent mumbled some choice curse words as she worked her small hand into his fly and sprang his flesh free. "Fuck," Kent snarled like a madman. "Fucking condom. Right front pocket. Hurry, baby. For the love of God, hurry."

Angie reluctantly released him, fished the foil-covered necessity out, then fumbled it open and on. She took her time making sure the damn thing was covering him good and tight, so much so that he was seriously in danger of embarrassing himself. Then she guided him past the skimpy panties to her entrance. They both groaned as he let her weight settle her onto him fully. Kent shook with the force of what he was feeling.

"I wanted it to be sweet our first time." He pulled out, lifted her up, then let her fall and thrust up at the same time. "I wanted it to be romantic for you."

Again he eased almost all the way out, lifting her, only to slam her back down. And again. Slow retreat, fast, hard advance. Then it was too much to try to control, and he braced her against the side of the car and let his hips fly, fast, hard, endless. It was maddening, it was mindless. It was sublime. She felt like she was designed by God just to fit him and he couldn't get enough. He wanted to pound inside her until they were fused and it was a fire consuming his soul.

Angie clutched at his shoulders and back then plunged her fingers into his hair. He wanted her to claw and scratch and cling and never stop. Kent felt the orgasm coming on like a gathering storm as her breath backed up in her lungs. That long, dark, shining hair of hers spilled down her back when she arched her spine and whispered, "I'm coming. I'm coming."

She looked up at him and he froze when he noticed her glasses had somehow managed to stay on. She peeked at him over them and he didn't need her whispered, "Come with me."

Because that was all it took for him, what he'd fantasized about since the first time she'd looked at him that way; he erupted. He couldn't call it an orgasm—it was too powerful for that. His entire body felt like it exploded and his hips slammed against her with a force he had never before used. A small part of his brain worried that he'd hurt her. He was unable to stop, though, as it went on and on. With the first hot tremor, she screamed into his chest to muffle the sound of her own climax as it clutched her flesh around his shaft in pulsating glory.

The parking lot was deserted and surrounded by trees on three sides and the river on the fourth. They were parked in a dimly lit back corner of it with no other cars in sight. Kent had parked there to keep his doors protected from the careless dings of other car doors. He wouldn't have started this with her if he'd thought they would be seen. He wouldn't have done this if he'd known about the audience they had. If he had known that the killer watched. And plotted.

Chapter Nine

Terryn's body was covered in a fine sheen of sweat. Her muscles, every blessed one of them, strained and trembled, laboring toward the climax that Brice continued to deny her. Her red hair was a tangle of wet ropes across her face and the drenched pillow beneath her. The imported Italian sheets were just as wet and tangled as her hair. And the man looming above her had become her entire world. He'd led her to this bed three hours ago. Then he'd tied her to it. Her arms were attached to the top two bedposts, her legs he'd left free. What followed was the most intense, complete and systematic exploration of her body that she could've imagined. And they hadn't even made love yet.

"Please," she panted in a voice gone hoarse with passion. "Please, Sir. Please…I can't. Oh God! I can't. I'm gonna come!"

"No," Brice commanded, his own body covered in sweat, his own voice gone ragged. "You won't come until I give you permission. Fight it." His hand was coated in the nectar her body gave up for him like a gift. He twisted the two fingers he was using on her so that the next pump in brushed her g-spot. When he felt the clench of her muscles that let him know she was starting to come, he pulled them out.

"I told you no." His hand just lay against her swollen flesh, not moving, just holding tight to her, and her head whipped back and forth on the pillow.

"Please. Please," she pleaded in a whisper, "I can't take it. Oh...just..." She tried to pump her hips up, hoping to get his fingers to move on her. "Just...anything. I don't care. I'll do anything. Just please!" Then her back arched and she screamed in passionate frustration.

Brice growled, she hoped because he was about to snap the leash he had on his control. "Oh, baby," he said, "you will do anything. Anything I say. Because this,"—he cupped his hand tight to her core—"this is mine." He leaned his head down to flick her nipple with the tip of his tongue. "Tell me. Tell me whose pretty pussy this is and I'll let you come."

Terryn had never thought she was into dirty talk. Frankly, words like "pussy" and "cock" always sounded vulgar to her whenever she heard them. Until Brice. Brice had been talking dirty to her from the second he'd touched her and she loved every word that came out of his mouth. Each time he said those taboo words, it only racked up her desire for more.

"Oh, Bri...Sir, yours." Her head lifted off the pillow so she breathed her next words across his lips. "It's all yours."

With a feral curse, Brice slipped his longest finger into her puckered back hole, all the way in, hard. She screamed and arched again until only her shoulders and heels were touching the mattress and he swore savagely as he watched her come. He had exploited every one of her erogenous zones, wringing three orgasms from just breast play alone before he'd moved on. She'd lost count of the number of orgasms he'd taken from her core. All she knew was that her very sanity balanced on giving him one more and then one more after that and more again until the universe narrowed down to only this room, this bed and this man.

When her body flopped back to the mattress, he lunged down and locked his mouth on to her dripping sheath, with his tongue delving deep. His finger kept thrusting in her ass, the muscles there clenching and pulsing just like the rest of her. This was the most turned on she could ever remember being and she was sure her mind was going to snap under the glorious weight of it. He stopped to rub his forehead on the inside of her thigh, gasping.

"God," he swore. "You fucking taste amazing." He hummed as he leaned in to take another savoring lick up the length of her core. "It must be the color of your hair or my imagination, but mmm." He swiped his tongue along her folds, like he was licking an ice-cream cone. "You taste like cinnamon and...mmm, brown sugar...and sex." He fastened his mouth again to her, while she writhed beneath him and every muscle in her body geared up for another explosion.

"It's pumpkin pie," she told him.

He stopped and murmured, "It sure is, baby, your sweet auburn hair does make it my pumpkin pie." Then he nibbled on the crease of her thigh where the scent of warm spices was strong, making her squirm.

"No," she whispered, too far gone to be embarrassed. "It's my body wash and lotion. It's actually called Pumpkin Pie."

He smiled like the Cheshire cat. "I love that. Now every Thanksgiving you are going to blush because you'll think of this and know that yours is the pumpkin pie I wish I were eating." And then he took the soft knot of her clit between his lips and ruthlessly worked his tongue over it until she blasted apart again.

Finally, he lifted his head. Terryn felt his muscles flex and tense as he maneuvered up her body and positioned himself between her limp thighs. She didn't think she had the strength to move or do anything but lay there passively after all the orgasms she'd had.

Then Brice said, "Terryn. Look at me." As soon as her eyes met his, he thrust.

She was so wet and ready for him, her body gave almost no resistance, and her flesh was so sensitized and primed from the hours of foreplay that she came from just that single thrust, groaning in rapture as he filled every part of her. Her muscles surged back to life, arms and legs straining as he pulled back and thrust again. His back flexed and his hips churned for several mind-blowing moments, then he braced his weight on one elbow next to her head. With his other hand he caught one leg and lifted it up and over his shoulder. The position opened her in a way that left her no defense, no way to limit his depth or speed. He took full advantage.

Terryn was held immobile as he pounded into her full force, pumping so deep and hard she was sure that she was going to blast into a million pieces. She did the only thing she was capable of, she closed her eyes and surrendered to the longest, most intense orgasm of her life, screaming.

Brice kept going, using every ounce of control and every trick he could think of to draw it out for her. As her walls continued to clench around him, he felt his control wrenching free of his will and his own orgasm hit him like a lightning strike. It struck at the base of his spine, boiled like fire in his sac and blasted out of him in shock waves. His head snapped back, his muscles spasmed and his hips powered into her like machine-gun fire. He shouted his release to the ceiling and rode out every jolt and tremor until the last lingering twitch had drifted from their bodies. Slowly, Brice lowered himself until his head was on the pillow next to hers. He hoped to hell he wasn't crushing her because he doubted he'd be able to move for a year.

Brice leaned back in his chair and steepled his fingers against his lips as he studied the murder board. Wrong thing to do if he wanted to concentrate on the case. He'd taken Terryn long into the night and when he woke for work this morning, he'd opted to have her one more time in the shower.

After their shower he mentioned his regret that she didn't smell like pie anymore and she'd smiled and handed him her purse. Inside was a travel-size bottle of her lotion and he'd covered every inch of her in it before he left. So, as his fingers were pressed to his face he could smell her on them.

It caused an instant reaction in his lap as well as skittering his thoughts back to the woman he'd left in an exhausted heap in the middle of his bed. He closed his eyes and basked for a moment. Allowing the raw images to flash like a movie reel through his mind while he took deep, savoring breaths rich with the lingering scent of cinnamon sugar-coated woman.

"Do you smell pumpkin pie?"

Brice cracked one eye open and looked at Kent, wondering if he was being serious or messing with him. Kent looked around, his expression similar to that of a kid waiting for Santa. Brice thanked his years on the force for being able to keep a straight face.

"Don't know what you're talking about, man." Brice sat up and shuffled papers, trying hard to look anywhere but at his partner as the guy craned his neck to look around the office.

Just when he was about to lose it and burst out laughing, Kent started to whistle. *Shit.* As the familiar tune of "Zip-a-Dee-Doo-Dah" happily sounded, Brice's laughter melted away to resignation. "Cut the crap for once, Kent," he said. "She's an A.D.A. when she's here, not your cousin. Give her some slack and show some respect."

"Yeah, Brandon," Ziporah Feldman said with a smirk "Why don't you grow up and cut me some slack?"

She and Kent had a love-hate relationship that went all the way back to the cradle. Brice didn't try to get in the middle of it often. The two fought and squabbled every time they came within shouting distance of each other. He had never seen two people who loved to fight as much as these two.

She was drop-dead sexy. All New York sleek, with mile-long legs and a figure that made every straight cop in the precinct do a double take. She had glossy brown hair that fell in a straight bob to her shoulders and big brown eyes that could drown a man or cut him in two depending on her mood. And she had the kind of wit that he knew brought his partner to his knees. Brice often wondered if Kent even realized that most of the women he dated were dead ringers for his cousin.

"Why would I want to do that when you're such an easy target, Zippy?" Kent smiled at her, obviously enjoying the signs of agitation she couldn't hide.

Ziporah tried to school her features and not show how much he irked her when he called her that. "You know damn well what my name is and if Ziporah is too hard for you, you can call me Ms. Feldman."

"Zip it for a minute, would you?" Kent interrupted and turned to look at Brice. Brice knew Kent could see her all but combust out of the corner of his eye. He also knew that it was everything his partner could do to keep a straight face. "Brice, did you call for the suit? If you did, I need to know. I mean, we're partners and I could've used some warning that the suits were descending on us today." He cut a look over his shoulder where his nemesis was all but fuming in her temper. "After all, if I'd known I would have dressed up."

"You're a moron. Aunt Betty should have traded you in for a puppy. How you made it to detective, I'll never know." Ziporah gave him a look that should have shriveled his balls and turned to Brice, deliberately turning her back on Kent. She laid the stack of files on his desk. "Here are the files you requested. Everything I could dig up on Brian Gwin and the girls at the Surf-N-Slurp. Not much there." She leaned close and looked deep into Brice's eyes. "You really think we got a serial killer here? If we do, you know you gotta turn it over to the feds."

Brice picked up the files and said, "I have no proof that we've got a serial on our hands. As soon as I do, you know Detective Kent and I will report it accordingly."

Ziporah smirked while Kent coughed "bullshit" into his fist and said, "Your captain loves you 'cause you always tie up your cases with a pretty bow for me. Same reason *I* love you, but you're walking a tight rope that could hang you if you're not careful." She patted his cheek as she straightened and walked away. "So be careful."

When Kent couldn't leave well enough alone and started whistling that obnoxious song again, she held up a choice finger for him without turning around. She repeated, "Moron," then turned the corner and headed for the elevator.

"So what files did you get zipped over here?" Kent asked.

"You know she's gone and can't hear you anymore, right?" When Kent just smirked, Brice answered, "I got her to dig up any juvenile records she could find on Gwin and the co-workers. It's a stretch but the best I could come up with at this point."

"Stretch is right. What the hell. Hand over one of those and let's get started." Kent opened Brian Gwin's file and asked, "Why does she love you enough to get you sealed records anyway? She wouldn't give me shit if I asked. And we share blood."

Brice couldn't believe the guy even asked. "Hmm, Kent, I don't know. Maybe it's because I don't act like a schoolyard bully every time she comes around."

"What?" Kent shocked him by being completely baffled. "I'm only playing with her. You don't think the teasing really bothers her, do you?" While Brice tried to come up with something more mature than the "duh" that he wanted to say, Kent shrugged and said, "Nah."

Brice let it go. There were more important things he could be doing than enlightening his partner.

Chapter Ten

Almost a full week later and they had learned very little that could lead them toward a killer. Brian Gwin had had some trouble. Mostly what you'd expect from a good-looking middle-class kid. Speeding tickets within a month of getting his license, underage drinking and partying. Pretty typical, harmless stuff.

The girls at the shop were a dead-end. Angie was an army brat who'd moved a lot yet still managed to pull in decent grades and keep her nose clean. Mandy had done time in a juvenile ward for underdeveloped or troubled kids—no surprise there considering how slow her mental faculties worked—but she'd kept out of trouble and stayed in school. Brice would be digging deeper into that anyway, just to be sure, but he wasn't expecting much. Jenny, the owner of the coffee shop, was squeaky clean. Youngest of five kids, married to her high school sweetheart and mother of three teenage girls. And every other file was just as much a dead-end as the last.

Brice let himself into his apartment with a million facts and images from the day still brewing in his mind. Terryn had his spare key and was going to be meeting him here any minute. He could not pull his head out of the case and focus on getting ready, even with the stop he'd made on the way home. He was so distracted with his thoughts that he'd taken three full steps into the living room before he saw her. Then he froze and abruptly forgot everything, including how to breathe.

Terryn knelt in the middle of the room with her head bowed. That radiant hair was pulled back in a tail that curled loosely down her back. Her knees were spread wide and her hands rested atop her thighs; one of them cradled a glass of wine. She was naked except for one thing.

A collar.

It wasn't from the club; it was white and had a gold heart-shaped loop dangling from its center. The fatigue, the strain and the stress of the day melted away as he studied her. His sub. The beauty of her at this moment was on level with a masterpiece. Light from the crystal chandelier glinted off her hair, making it glow as it brought out the many different hues of red that made it so breathtaking. Her lovely willowy body still showed the signs from last week's lovemaking. There were faint pink patches scattered from cheek to knees from his five-o'clock shadow. There were also a couple of faded bite marks and hickeys in some tantalizing places.

Looking at her like this, willingly submissive and awaiting his pleasure while covered with marks from his lovemaking, settled something in him that he'd been unaware needed settling. *This*, he thought to himself, *This is what Heaven would be like if I could design it.*

He stepped forward and brushed one finger down her cheek, "Is that wine for me, little sub?"

Terryn felt alive as she never had before. The only thing that kept the pain of Katie's loss away was focusing on what she had discovered about herself at the hands of Brice last week. When she and Katie had first started exploring BDSM, she had thought it sounded exciting. She pictured herself having an adventure. She also feared finding it a lot less glamorous than the books promised. Although she had hoped for the glamorous, she was prepared for lackluster at best and a painfully awkward embarrassment at worst. She'd never dreamed it would turn out to be her destiny.

She knew that Brice was a huge part of the reason everything was so perfect right now. She was never going back to the vanilla way of life. This is what she had been searching for. This is what had always been missing from every relationship she ever had. Now that she'd found it, it would never be missing again.

When it came to sex, she wanted to serve her Master. More importantly, she wanted to serve *this* Master. To please him. She wanted to give control of her body and pleasure over to his will. Whatever that may be. In this place of peace where she'd centered herself and cleared her mind of everything, she didn't think about all the logical reasons that said she was moving too fast. She couldn't hear the inner voices that would caution her to hold back. In this place, that pounding drive in her heart that told her he was everything she'd dreamed of was the only voice she heard.

Surviving in a big, overcrowded city was both fun and a challenge. She had to battle her way through one job after the next, even with her degree. Every chore, bill and duty was hers and hers alone. As she reflected back on it now, her previous relationships had been just another responsibility on top of all the others. They were for the most part decent guys who had seemed to truly care for her. Unfortunately Terryn could see now that she had steered clear of men that had any backbone at all. Too frightened of ending up in a relationship full of drama, she had chosen easygoing, mild-mannered men. And all of them had been just as passive in bed as out of it. Not uncaring of her, just not what she needed. In every other aspect of her life she had to make decisions. For the first time she found a way to let go. A safe place to let all the decisions and control rest in someone else's hands. Yeah, she was never going back.

With BDSM, she had no responsibility other than what her Dom desired. Terryn was free to let go. In this perfect moment, her mind was at peace. There was only a sense of safety and calm as she offered the wine she had prepared and whispered, "Yes, Sir."

The glass was lifted with one hand and he used his other to tilt her chin until she met his smoldering gaze. His lips parted and the deep red wine seemed to caress them as it passed into his mouth. His dark pink tongue came out before he lowered the glass to catch a drop that lingered on the edge. Watching a man take a drink had never been so erotic.

"Thank you, sub." His fingers brushed the sensitive skin under her chin while his thumb stroked lightly along her lips. "I'm glad you're here." Terryn could only nod as he took another tantalizing dink and continued to touch her. "I like the collar, but it's not mine. Take it off." With shaking fingers, Terryn released the clasp and dropped it to the side.

"From now on, you'll wear my collar and no other. Even at the club. Understood?"

Recognizing that for the claim of ownership it was caused Terryn's breath to catch on a gasp. Brice took advantage of her parted lips by sliding his thumb in. Without being told, Terryn locked her lips around the digit and started to worship it with her tongue and suck on it like a favorite candy treat. She was rewarded with a deep groan while he took another taste of wine. His thumb wasn't enough—she wanted more. *Needed* more.

She started to raise her hands and was stopped by his arched brow. Her eyes implored, and with another sip he nodded his consent. First the belt gave way, then the slacks and silk boxers, until finally he was hard and hot in her hands. Pulsing in her grasp. He was magnificent. She gripped the base and gave a firm pull all the way to the flared head then stroked back again. His hum of pleasure was like nourishment to her. When he slid his thumb from her mouth and guided her to his cock as he continued to enjoy his drink, she thought it was the sexiest thing she'd ever done.

His taste flowed into her senses the way the wine must have been flowing into his. The shaft was long and thick, the head so wide she feared catching it on her teeth. He controlled all the action as he slowly and steadily slid to the back of her throat. He held there, restricting her breathing, and Terryn concentrated on taking shallow breaths through her nose until he relented and slowly eased back out.

Nothing in her life seemed to matter as much as pleasing him, bringing him even a fraction of what he'd bestowed on her. Terryn pulled everything she'd ever read about blow jobs and every trick she'd ever learned into her mind and poured it all into motion. She licked and sucked and swirled and bobbed as he drank his wine and stroked her hair.

Before long, she noticed a tremor in his hand that then transferred to his legs. His breathing grew frantic and the hums of pleasure were morphing into deep growls of lust interspersed with phrases like, "Oh fuck, baby" and "God, that's good." Then, "Yeah, like that. Hmmm, harder. Suck me harder. Yeah."

Terryn had never enjoyed going down on a man more. As his moans got louder and his directions more coarse, her own desire climbed. She was dripping wet and as impossible as it seemed, she felt perilously close to an orgasm. That feeling only intensified when he fisted his hand in her hair and started thrusting, wrenching control away once more.

Her hips flexed in time with the thrusts into her mouth and her own moans now mingled in the air with his and suddenly, with a deep reverberating shout, he came. The first stream fired into her mouth with surprising force, followed by another and another as he flexed and pumped and Terryn gasped in enchanted surrender as she came too. Without any direct contact to any part of her body below the chin, she came in a wonderful rush of heat and her nails dug tiny crescents into his thighs as she rode out both their climaxes to the sweet, blissful end.

As Brice slipped out of Terryn's mouth, she nuzzled and sipped at him, cleaning him as he withdrew. It was thorough enough that he was still hard when he put his clothes back in order. That had to have been the best oral he'd ever gotten. He felt as though his legs were going to give out any minute and he didn't think he cared. His little sub was looking up at him with a flush of arousal on her cheeks and stars in her eyes.

He ran his thumb along her cheekbone and said, "I'm going to put something on you for tonight and then we are going to have dinner at my cousin's place." He searched her expression for signs that he was moving her too fast. "Let me know if you aren't ready for this. Say 'pickles' now or else know that you will be coming as my sub tonight."

He watched as Terryn processed what he said. He didn't see fear or even caution, he saw eagerness. With a sensuous curve of her spine, she bowed down until her lips caressed the top of his foot and said, "I am yours to command. Yours to use in any way you see fit." She turned her face just enough to let them make eye contact. "Master." Brice took a deep steadying breath in order to rein in the urge to simply forget his plans and ravage her right then.

He stepped back instead and reached for the briefcase he'd left by the front door. "This is a little device I picked up on my way home." He pulled out the package and held it up for her to see. When her eyes widened and her mouth made a little "o" of shock, he grinned from ear to ear. This was going to be fun.

"Stand up and clasp your hands behind your head." Once she did, he started attaching the device as he explained, "First the belt—it has the receiver for the remote and all the wires connect from here. Next, your nipples." They were already tightly puckered, which made this part easy. He squirted the reactive jelly onto the pads, then centered each one directly over the aroused tips.

As he connected the wires from the belt to the pads, he asked, "Have you ever had a medical test done where they measure your heart or reflexes? This works in a similar way. Every time I press the remote, it will trigger these little pads, like this." He hit one of the buttons on the remote and watched as it flexed on her right breast. Terryn gasped and started to drop her arms.

"Keep your hands where I've put them, sub." He used a firm voice, his Dom voice, and Terryn reacted instantly by snapping back into position. "Do you like that?" he asked and hit the button for her other breast.

She jerked and her knees wobbled, but she kept her hands in place and nodded. "Yes, Sir. I do."

He knew from what he'd read about this pricey little toy that the breast and clit pads would move like little sucking mouths where they were placed. The electrical current caused the pads to contract and flex over those sensitive bits of flesh and with the medical-grade adhesive holding them in place, it promised to be an exciting evening no matter how wet or active she became.

"Spread your legs for me." She did with a whimper. "Wider. Nice. Now hold very still." He knelt and spread her labia. "Damn, you are so wet." He leaned forward and took a savoring lick. "We have to have you dry for the adhesive to work though."

Brice riffled around in his briefcase until he came up with a napkin left from his lunch takeout. Then he gently and thoroughly dried her clit and the flesh surrounding it. With careful fingers, he made sure that the pad was placed exactly as it should be, with the hood pulled back to expose the ultra-sensitive tissues. He took extra care that nothing was pinching uncomfortably.

"That looks perfect." He looked up at her with one eyebrow arched. "Shall we test this one too?" He hit the remote and was savagely pleased when she responded with a deep, guttural shout of pleasure. Even braced for it, she still stumbled in place for a brief second before she righted herself. Brice kept his eyes on her face when he pulled out the next piece. He wasn't disappointed; she gulped and looked ready to panic at the sight of the vibrator.

Before he slid it into place, he ran it in light circles around both her holes, just to keep her guessing which it was going to be in for the night. He slid the small shaft halfway in to her weeping pussy and rotated it a couple times. Her knees threatened to buckle and her hips flexed, but her arms were still where he'd ordered them to stay. He pulled it out and ran it over each silky lip, then tapped the tip against her covered clitoris. Terryn's entire body jolted with each teasing touch.

When he slipped it back to toy and press on her untried ass she gave a low purr of pleasure. He watched her face carefully for signs of discomfort as he pressed until the very tip popped in. Her gasp and whimper were all the encouragement he needed.

"Mmm, that's nice. Now, little sub, turn around, bend over and spread your pretty cheeks for me." He could seat it from here with no problem, but he wanted her to open herself for it. He wanted his sub to submit for him and show him she willingly took what he wanted to give her. Without saying another word, Brice twirled one finger in the air, motioning for her to turn. She did it—with shaking hands and a tremor in her legs—but she did it.

He almost drooled at the sight. The skin was flushed with arousal, the deep pink color of her pussy fading to a blush around her anus. He took time to stroke the toy over her lips and pump it an inch into her sheath for a few seconds before sliding up to circle and tease the smaller hole. He leaned forward, no longer able to resist, and used his tongue there, lapping and suckling while pulsing the plug in and out before finally gliding it home. The anal plug was small in both diameter and length, so it slid into place with ease while Terryn gasped and moaned.

He helped her stand back up and checked again to make sure nothing pinched or pulled, then told her to go and dress for dinner. As she did that, Brice went and got himself cleaned up as well. Anticipation hummed pleasantly through his veins. This promised to be a night to remember.

Chapter Eleven

Terryn had never been to the restaurant adjacent to the club. It held a five-star rating according to *Forbes Travel Guide*, and that was a little too spendy for her. She figured she'd have to make a lot more money than she currently did to justify dropping three digits for a single meal.

Brice helped her out of the cab and led her right past the line and into the lobby. A handsome young man with dark features looked up and literally beamed when he spotted them. "Detective," he greeted as he swung out from behind the maître d' podium. "I have your table set and ready. Cade and Trevor left orders for me to call as soon as you arrived."

Brice shook his hand. "Terryn, I'd like you to meet Mike. Mike, this is Terryn."

Terryn smiled and shook his offered hand. He had kind eyes and a gentle touch. Terryn liked him instantly and poured a little more warmth into her smile. It froze on her face when an instant buzzing flared to life in her ass and on her clit. She locked her knees and tried desperately not to let her face reflect what was going on below her waist.

Mike, either oblivious or tactful, turned and led them toward a table. She turned a glare in Brice's direction. Big mistake. Both her breasts immediately felt as though they were being sucked, vigorously. Brice gave her his Dom face, all stern and foreboding until she schooled her features and managed to wipe the glare away.

"You wanna tell me why you did that?" she squeaked as she struggled to keep from collapsing on the way to their table.

"You were flirting."

Her gasp was loud and immediate. It also earned her a higher speed on the butt plug. "I wasn't flirting; you're just using that as an excuse." The smug grin he didn't bother to hide gave truth to her claim. "All I did was smile at him."

Brice didn't stop grinning but he turned off the toys and caressed a hand along her arm. "Honey, you've gotta be careful with those smiles. A look like that from a woman like you—well, it could ruin a man. Turn him into a lovesick idiot if you're not careful." Even though they were talking in whispers and Mike gave no indication that he could hear them, Terryn felt her face heat with embarrassment.

As if proving his point, Mike pulled out Terryn's chair himself and even unfolded her napkin with extra flourish. When he tried to place it in her lap as well, Brice had enough and snapped out a request that he hurry and call his cousin. Terryn hid her smile with her water glass and all but hummed with joy. It was nice to have a man be possessive of her.

"So," she said, "I thought we were going to have dinner at your cousin's place." Not that she minded the nice restaurant; she was just trying to make conversation.

"We are."

Brice watched her with a strange, expectant look in his eye. Like dominoes falling into place, she put it all together. If this was his cousin's place, then that meant the club was too. And that meant that his cousin knew she had joined the club. She gasped as the last piece fit. That meant that Trevor and Riley also had to know. Her bosses.

Brice must have recognized that the look on her face was dread because he leaned close and whispered, "They own the place, Red. Think about it. Why would someone own a fetish club unless they were at least open to the lifestyle?" He laid a gentle kiss on her temple and murmured, "You already know they are a threesome. They'd be no more than hypocrites to have a problem with you being a member here."

It helped a little when he put it that way. "I know, but they are my bosses. I have to work with them every day. How can I face them knowing they know I like...um..." She looked around and leaned closer to whisper, "What I like."

Brice, the beast, only chuckled and turned the breast cups back on. It was incredible the way the little suction cups felt like mouths. With the gel he'd squirted into each before applying them, it was even wet. She let out a soft moan and felt her eyes drift close, forgetting the worry and allowing herself to just enjoy the sensation.

"Now there's a pretty sight." Terryn's eyes popped open at the sound of Trevor's voice. He was looking at her with frank appreciation.

"Mmm, I'd have to agree." Cade walked up with a stunning Riley under one arm. Riley gave her a coconspirator's grin while Cade looked Terryn over with a familiar glint in his eye. She'd seen the same expression on Brice's face a hundred times since they'd come together.

"So, Brice," Cade said without taking his eyes off Terryn, "I see you took our advice and picked up the tool belt. It's put a lovely flush on your sub's face and a sheen in her eyes that's quite becoming."

"I'll have to agree with you there, Cade," Brice said as he rose and gave each one in turn that warm, one-armed guy hug that all men seem to know. Before he sat back down, he placed a soft kiss on Riley's cheek, then resumed his seat next to Terryn. Before she could say anything herself, Riley reached across the table and clasped one of Terryn's hands in both of hers.

"Terryn," she began, making eye contact and never breaking it. "I am so glad you wanted to come tonight. I was worried that you might feel awkward or something silly like that. We want you to know that this changes nothing about work. We love you. The center wasn't half of what it is now that you've come along and brought so much to it." She gave Terryn's hand another encouraging squeeze before sitting between her two men.

"Outside of work," said Brice in his Dom tone, "especially in the club or at a time like this when you are here as my sub, you will give them the respect and accord that you would any Dom." One strong hand tilted her chin up and over until she was looking him in the eye. "Understood?"

She should have been livid. She should have stormed out. She should've at least been mortified. What she felt, though, was incredibly turned on. To keep from moaning, Terryn caught her bottom lip between her teeth and tried to focus on her breathing in order to distract herself from the need that was raging through her veins like a virus.

She must not have answered fast enough because the vibrations on her clit shot back on right then and her whole body jerked in reaction. Brice kept her chin gripped tight in his fingers and his intense stare wouldn't allow her eyelids to droop closed like she wanted them to. Her body gave a sharp jerk and tried to curl in on itself as an orgasm bloomed to life and burst over her. She couldn't stop the panting whimpers that spilled from between her parted lips as Brice alternated the speed and strength of the toys, prolonging her pleasure. The whole time, his eyes never left her face and the look in those eyes left no doubt in Terryn's mind that this—*she*—was pleasing him.

Terryn heard a soft gasp and looked across the table at Riley. Brice laid a quick and plundering kiss on her lips before he reluctantly released her. When Terryn met Riley's eyes, she felt a renewed rush of desire. Riley was flushed and panting. She was trying her best not to show it, but having just experienced it herself, Terryn could tell Riley was trying to hold back her own climax. Her hands were out of sight, but Terryn could see the muscles in her arms flexing, leading Terryn to assume she was quite literally trying to get a grip on herself. Terryn looked from Cade to Trevor. Both men were acting as though nothing unusual was going on and Trevor even gave her a wink as he lifted his glass for a drink.

"I took the liberty of ordering our meal ahead of time. I hope you don't mind," Cade said to Brice, who assured him he'd expected nothing less. Terryn opened her mouth to ask Cade what they were doing to Riley and two things happened at once. The butt plug flared to sudden blaring life and Brice gripped a fistful of hair at the back of her neck.

He looked casual and relaxed, talking to her with hardly any eye contact. "Terryn, a sub doesn't address a Dom without first gaining permission from her own Dom. If we were here on a normal night out, which will be the case often, I'm sure, you may speak as freely as you please. But like we've already covered, you are here as my sub this evening and unless the word coming out of your mouth was 'pickles', you were about to overstep your bounds."

She gulped and nodded. As an afterthought, she also lowered her eyes and tried to sound contrite as she murmured an apology. Contrite was hard to do when what you felt was a whirlwind of excitement, lust and adventure. She heard another sound of pleasure from Riley and this time it was accompanied by a sharp nudge of her foot under the table.

Terryn, still trying for contrite, peeked through her lashes to see what was going on. Riley clearly hadn't meant to nudge her; it was obvious that she was losing her fight to hold off her orgasm. She was shifting restlessly in her seat and now had a firm visible grip on the arms of her men. They continued to enjoy their drinks and pretend that they had no clue that their wife was about to implode.

Suddenly, Riley slumped and relaxed in her seat. She blew out a little huff and eyed each of her men in turn before she said in a hiss, "That was just mean." Trevor smirked and Cade only arched a brow as Riley then looked at Terryn and said, "They do this to me all the time. Get me so worked up I'm about to blow and then stop before I can." She gave another huff and glared at them again.

Cade said, "The food is coming, Ry. We were trying to save you from 'blowing' in front of Mike." He smiled in a dazzling display of teeth and added, "But, if you'd rather we continue..." Riley was quick to shake her head and give him big pleading eyes as Mike did indeed appear just then, wheeling a tray of food.

"Riley is wearing the tool belt as well, Terryn," Brice whispered while Mike placed plates filled with food that looked more like art in front of everybody.

Terryn's head snapped up and she gaped at Riley who nodded and gave her a mischievous wink very similar to the one Trevor had given her a moment ago. They smiled at each other and Terryn felt a connection to Riley that she hadn't felt with another woman besides Katie.

A sharp pain stabbed her heart at the thought and for a moment Terryn felt guilty for feeling anything other than grief.

It seemed wrong to be happy when her friend was gone. Her eyes started to fill and then Riley reached out across the table.

"I miss her too. It's so awful that we'll never get to see her again." Riley's eyes teared up as well and Terryn felt that connection go even deeper. Three days ago, Terryn would have slid into her grief and drowned in the sorrow engulfing her, with no one close to turn to and nothing to distract her from the pain. She'd just flailed under the relentless waves that crashed upon her like the sea during a storm.

Now, she focused outside herself and gripped Riley's hands tightly. "She loved you guys," she said to them in a voice that was husky with the effort it took to hold back the tears. "She never told me about anything personal or intimate. She had more class than to betray a confidence. But she did talk about the non-personal stuff and she thought the world of you all."

Trevor made a sound in his throat that was a cross between a grunt and a sigh, yet it conveyed a wealth of emotion held in check. Cade acknowledged the words with a nod of thanks and tucked a curl of Riley's dark hair behind her ear, then cupped the back of her neck in his palm to comfort her.

Riley absorbed the warmth for a moment, then seemed to take herself in hand with a shake of her head and gave Terryn's hands one last squeeze before sitting back and picking up her wine. "Well," she said as she lifted the glass, "tonight isn't a night for sadness. Let's give her a toast and then we'll put it away."

As all them lifted and clinked glasses with a chorus of, "To Katie," Terryn felt that Katie would be touched and the thought was comforting enough that she *could* put it away—for now.

The meal was light and delicious. Before Terryn started she was sure she was going to have to choke down the food. Too much emotion and nerves always killed her appetite. She just hoped she'd be able to eat enough to be polite. After that first bite, however, Terryn felt her hunger awaken and the meal became a delicate feast.

The men spoke of family issues and shared past stories, each trying to one-up the others with childhood tales. Riley and Terryn were both charmed and laughing before the second course was served. Terryn was more than a little shocked to realize that she was dating a rich man when she'd thought she was dating a cop. The stories they told involved exotic places, yachts and even servants. Things Terryn had only seen in movies or read about in books.

"Small family inheritance, huh?" she teased after a particularly funny story about how the three of them had gotten kicked out of a British boarding school.

Brice only arched a brow and said, "I had more on my mind at that moment than my portfolio. If memory serves, so did you."

Terryn grinned and had to give him that one.

Brice watched as Terryn lost the sadness. It was like watching a flower bloom. She was wide open and vibrant with life and laughter. As dessert was served, he signaled Cade and Trevor.

Terryn took her first bite of chocolate mousse and he hit the switch that activated her breasts. She fumbled her spoon a little and as she wiped a dab of chocolate from her chin, she sent him a glare. Just like he'd hoped she would—it gave him the excuse to activate the anal plug. Her eyes widened and a flush stole up her neck to heat her face. He felt an answering heat settle in his groin as he watched her.

When he looked over at Riley, he could tell her men had activated something on her as well. While the conversation between him and the other two men turned to the upcoming fundraiser to benefit both centers, the women fell silent. Both grew flushed and it became apparent that neither of them were going to hold out for long and the mood shifted from lighthearted to needy.

"Did you manage to tap the senator for a speech again this year?" Brice asked as he slid a hand along Terryn's thigh.

He tugged a little until she got the message and spread her legs for him while Trevor told him about some guests lined up for the event. She'd followed directions and had no underwear on to navigate around, so when Brice continued his journey up her leg he found nothing but hot, wet woman. He traced the soft petals of her core lightly, tickling strokes that added to the sensations already bombarding her. She squirmed in her seat and tried to angle her hips to entice him inside and he stopped the motion with a sharp pinch on one labia. Her whole body jolted and a sexy gasp left her lips. God, he loved the sounds she made.

"So, gentlemen," Brice said, "shall we continue this in the penthouse?"

"Hey, y'all, is this a private party?" Five seconds ago Brice would have said that nothing short of murder could have distracted him at that moment. He would have been wrong.

Brice pulled his hand back from Terryn and stood to hug his oldest and dearest friend. "Gage," he said, thumping him on the back. "Damn, it's good to see you, man."

Gage was a good three inches taller than he was and had the thick build of a pro football player. Since Brice was six-two and no lightweight, it always shocked him a little when he was up close and personal with him. The big Texan pounded him a couple times between his shoulders and if Brice hadn't been braced for it, he would've been toppled into the table.

"Why didn't you tell us you were coming?" Brice asked.

Gage gave him a last bone-crushing squeeze and stepped around the table to thump on the other two men. "Well, I wasn't plannin' on comin'. You know me. I got an itch to see ya and decided to scratch it." He turned to Riley who'd been bouncing on her toes waiting for her turn to hug him. "C'mere, l'il dahrlin'." He swung her up and cradled her like he was holding an infant. Brice smirked and thought she looked like one in his arms.

"We miss you." Riley kissed his cheek and wrapped her arms around his neck.

"Aw, now, dahrlin', that's nice to hear." He smiled fondly at her, then grinned at her husbands, "Well now, I got what I came here for, so I'll be seein' ya." He turned as if to leave, but Cade stood up and plucked Riley from his hold with a chuckle.

"Nice try, Gage. I keep telling you—not until we're dead. You know we left her to you in the will."

"You might want to stop reminding me," Gage said as he stole a chair from a nearby table and sat down. "See, my best friend o'er there is a cop and he might get suspicious when you two turn up missin'."

Brice knew the second Gage became aware of Terryn. The easygoing, smooth-talking Texan disappeared in a blink to be replaced by two hundred plus pounds of hungry Dom. Gage was more of a sucker for a redhead than Brice was and Terryn was no ordinary redhead.

He stared at her for a full thirty seconds, taking in every detail as she squirmed in her seat, trying to keep still. Brice could tell she was nervous about this unexpected turn of events and he felt a swell of pride in his chest that she stayed true to the rules of the evening.

"Brice, my friend," Gage said, his already deep baritone voice even deeper now, "please tell me you are not as selfish with this sweet treasure as these two are with theirs."

Brice watched Terryn closely as he twirled a lock of her hair around one finger and answered. "You know me."

He left it at that to see how she'd react when he didn't clarify. He'd mentioned sharing her briefly on the night they'd met and the thought had turned her on. He had been planning on exploring that later. Now with Gage here, it was just too easy. The only men he trusted more as Doms were Cade and Trevor.

She was being a good little sub and continued to wait on his Will, so he'd cut the suspense early. "Terryn," he said, leaning close to whisper hot and quiet in her ear, "this is my closest friend. He's also one of the best Doms I've ever seen in action. Why don't you go say hello?" Then he kissed the side of her neck and sat back. Gage was seated across from them with his legs sprawled wide and his focus never wavered as Terryn stood up and walked to him.

"Damn, son." Gage said it like a prayer when she rounded the table and he got a clear look at her from head to foot.

Brice had to give her credit—she didn't falter. She just walked right up to him and with her head lowered whispered, "Hello, um, Sir. I'm Terryn."

Gage looked once more toward Brice for confirmation— which Brice thought was only right—and only after he received a nod of approval did he reach out and touch her. He scooped a hand under her hair and another around her hips, then pulled until she was flush against his side. Then he kissed her.

Brice had been braced for it, sure that he would feel a tidal wave of jealousy. But what he felt was a fierce rush of heat. That was his sub and she was blowing his friend's mind right now with just a kiss. Brice could see Gage's hand clinch where it rested on her hip. She stood back from his kiss on shaky legs, but Gage only tightened his hold and tugged her into his lap. With all the things that they could do to her dancing through his imagination, Brice decided that it was time to call an end to dinner.

"Well," he said to Cade and the others, "I think our plans have changed for the evening. We'll have to continue this another time."

Brice knew that they all loved Gage like family, but he also knew that he himself was still the only man they allowed in during a scene with Riley. Brice could count on one hand the number of times they'd had her in the playrooms at the club and during those times no one was allowed into the play. It was strictly hands-off.

"Bring him around tomorrow when you surface. We'll shoot a couple rounds of pool and catch up." Cade then stood and took Riley by the hand. "Come on, Ry, Trevor and I are not through playing with you yet."

Riley leaned over to kiss Gage and Terryn both on the cheek before the two men ushered her up and away. After only a couple steps, she stopped and hurried back to give Brice a hug. The gesture warmed his heart.

"You be careful not to let Gage steal her away," she whispered, for his ears alone. "I think she just might be the one for you."

Brice smiled and whispered back, "What makes you think that?"

She laid a soft kiss on his cheek and said, "Because you didn't ask me to run away with you this time." Then she sauntered back to her men. If she would have turned to face him, he wondered if she'd be surprised to see the dumbstruck look he could feel on his face.

"So, dahrlin'." Gage pulled her tighter into his lap and Brice looked over to see her face flush when she met his eyes. "Before we get started, I need to know your safe word."

"'Pickles', Sir," Terryn said and turned a fiery red when Gage laughed full and loud.

"Wh-why in God's green earth did you pick that?" he managed to gasp out between chuckles.

"Yes," Brice added with a smile and a chuckle of his own. "Why pickles?" He sat back down and decided to let Riley's unsettling comment go until he had time to give it serious thought.

"Well." Terryn couldn't face them as she explained her choice, so she fiddled with a fold in her skirt and answered. "I wanted to pick something that could never be mistaken for a sex word." She laughed herself and continued, "You know, something that would never be called out during sex under any circumstance."

"You succeeded, sugar." Gage then stood her on her feet and said to Brice, "Let's dance a while first. I got a need to show you up on the dance floor before we get started."

Brice stood back up and gestured for Gage to lead the way. "Dance all you want, twinkle-toes," he taunted. "It won't make a damn bit of difference. She's mine."

Chapter Twelve

Terryn was having the time of her life.

Gage laughed and smiled constantly. Terryn couldn't help but stare at the big man. The Texan was taller than anyone she had ever danced with and his shoulders and arms were huge. He also had a tight, rock-hard abdomen; she knew because he kept dragging her up against it. He was handsome as a pirate, all dressed in black from head to toe, and he was beautiful in a way very few men were. He wasn't pretty, not like a man who looked too feminine. Rather, he was how she pictured an avenging angel would appear. He had amazing bone structure, piercing blue eyes and thick, wavy blond hair that he had tied at the back of his neck. She was the envy of every woman in the club.

He also hadn't let her leave the dance floor since they'd walked onto it. Terryn was more than impressed with his skill—she was dazzled. He moved with a powerful grace and commanded her every step with such ease she felt like she was floating. She'd never danced with a guy who could lead so masterfully and it made something hot and needy come to life in her belly.

Brice wasn't dancing. He was seated at a table close to the dance floor and watched them with a gleam in his eye that let her know he was enjoying what he saw. Terryn felt as strong of a connection with him right then as she did with Gage. She felt like she was dancing for Brice and every move she made, every sway of her body was for his pleasure and entertainment.

Gage grabbed her hips and turned her 'til her back was flush to his front, then he bent his knees until she felt the bulge of his erection nestled against her ass. He gave a hard thrust and pulled her tight to him at the same time and right then Brice brought the clit stimulator to life.

"Let's see how long it takes to get our boy there outta his chair, hmm?" Gage whispered huskily in her ear.

Then those large, calloused hands started running all over her body. He dipped low and cupped a hand around each knee then straightened slowly, his hands dragging up the inside of her legs the whole way. When he reached the tops of her thighs, he pulled her hips back into his again and then set them on a grinding, sensuous rotation that had her panting and him hard as granite between her cheeks.

Her arms moved with a will of their own, sliding her hands over the large ones that gripped her thighs, then up over her swaying body. She cupped her breasts, caressing them like an offering to Brice.

"Mmm, dahrlin'," Gage rumbled in her ear. "That's it. Tease those sweet thangs for us. Damn." His voice dropped even lower when she ground her ass harder against him. His head dipped and he set his teeth to the ultra-sensitive spot where neck met shoulder—and bit. A shock wave seared over her body from that spot out and Terryn arched her head back onto Gage with a strangled moan.

Terryn hadn't realized that her eyes had closed until they flew open when Brice joined them. His face was stark with desire as he settled his hands on her hips. She had assumed he couldn't dance since he'd been watching up until now but when he brought himself flush to her front and started moving with them, she realized that she was wrong. Brice moved with the same primitive animal grace that he made love with. He placed one strong leg between her thighs, one hand on her waist and circled his hips against hers.

Gage laughed low in his chest, the sound of an aroused man who knew he was getting what he wanted, and moved in perfect sync with Brice. They shifted forward and back and up and down and the whole time there were hands on her everywhere. Gage slid one up the back of her thigh to grab a full cheek of her ass in a caress that stole the breath from her. Brice lifted her arms up and back 'til they draped over Gage's shoulders, then trailed his hands from her elbows to her breasts while the three of them swayed into a graceful arch.

Terryn didn't know how many people in the club were watching and she wouldn't have cared if she did. They mastered her body on that floor the way she longed to be mastered in bed and she was lost in the erotic thrill of it.

Just when she was so turned on she wouldn't have cared if they stripped her and took her right there on the dance floor, Gage turned her around and lifted her in one fluid move. Before she knew what had happened, she had her legs tight around his hips and his hands were grinding her against him as he and Brice headed for the playrooms. Gage's hands were so large that he completely engulfed the cheeks of her ass. Once they were far enough in the hallway to be out of sight from the main club, he let those hands get busy.

"Well, well, well," he said in that sexy southern drawl. "Lookie what we have here." One long finger found the anal plug. Terryn let out a squeak as he started pushing it in deeper in rhythm with his steps.

She heard Brice say, "I wondered when you'd find that." Then Brice turned it on.

Terryn didn't squeak then—she *shouted*. Every muscle in her body flexed and pulsed in time with what Gage was doing. His steps slowed and he pulled his head back a little to watch her face as she grew more and more frantic.

He murmured words of encouragement to her, telling her to come, telling her, "Get it, girl. C'mon, lemme see it. Lemme feel it" in a voice so gravelly deep just the sound alone could have made her come.

But it wasn't just his voice, it was that fantastic body he'd been teasing her with for the last hour and his hands on her and the toys that Brice kept turning off and on. Terryn locked so tightly against him she would have feared choking him if she had a brain cell capable of functioning right then. She buried her face in the curve of his neck and exploded in one of the most powerful orgasms she'd ever experienced while she quivered and shook in his embrace.

Gage's body seemed to turn to stone under and around her. He cupped one hand behind her head while the other doubled the pace of the plug as he let fly with a string of cuss words and erotic promises while the orgasm laid waste to her system.

Terryn felt Brice's arms come around her and he gently pulled her free. She wobbled when he stood her on her feet, so Brice opted to carry her instead. He cradled her in his arms like she was the proverbial damsel of a fairy tale. She felt like one at the moment. With an inner purr, she amended that it was an X-rated fairy tale, which only made it that much better to her way of thinking.

Gage led them to the check-in area, but Terryn only had eyes for Brice at the moment. His features looked carved in granite and his smoldering gaze made her feel singed.

"That was the sexiest thing I've ever seen, pet." His arms tightened even more. "I need you to promise to use your safe word if you feel too overwhelmed. Promise me, because as soon as we get you to a room," he took a deep breath, visibly straining for control, "that's the only thing that's going to stop us, Terryn. The only thing."

Terryn would have liked to say something coy in reply. Something flirty and sophisticated that would make her sound worldly and urbane. Looking at him in that moment, feeling the waves of lust and heat pouring off him peeled away all her outer layers and left only what she was at her core. A submissive.

"I promise, Sir." Then she lowered her eyes.

I promise, Sir. Brice felt the words reverberating in his soul. Her surrender, her submission went to his head like whisky and sang through his blood like a drug. He called on every control technique he had at his disposal to rein in the beast within while Gage checked them in.

"Master Gage!" The breathy call that came from the young woman behind the counter. It was filled with the zealous glee usually heard only by rock stars. In this club, however, it was the Master Doms that were the rock stars and of them, Gage was legendary. Brice tore his gaze from Terryn and watched with a smile while the normally reserved and properly quiet Candy bounced on the balls of her feet and reached with both hands toward Gage. "It's been so long since you came. Are you going to be staying for a while? Have you picked a sub for your stay? Can I help? Can I be your—"

"Well now, sugar," Gage interrupted, crossing his arms over his massive chest, purposefully reminding her that a sub doesn't touch without permission. He gentled the rebuke with his ever-present smile and said, "I'm just in for a short visit, and me an' Master Brice there are fixin' to get us a playroom. Can you be a dahrlin' and sign us in?"

Candy's hopeful face fell faster than a popped balloon and Brice felt a pang of sympathy. Candy was such an earnest, sweet sub, and her crush on Gage was obvious. Brice whispered to Terryn and set her on her feet so he could put his things in his locker, then they headed for their room. Once he closed the door behind them, he felt his blood simmer back up to boil.

"Strip," Brice said as he crossed his arms over his chest and leaned back against the door. Gage's smile was sharp and quick as he too crossed his arms and stood back to watch.

Terryn looked unsure for a moment. Then she took a deep breath and reached for the hem of her little black dress. Gage whistled low and soft as the gown fluttered to the floor.

Terryn stood in the middle of the room, anxious yet ready. She wore only the belt and a sexy pair of heels. The rosy tips of her perfect breasts were obscured under the pads that were attached to the belt. Likewise, her clit was also hidden from view with a pad and the scant covering of her most sensitive parts was as taunting as a red flag to a bull.

As she stood there with her shoulders back and spine straight, Brice was struck by her intensity as well as her beauty. It was a heady rush having a strong woman waiting on his Will.

"Gage." With the tilt of his head, Brice indicated the bar hanging from the ceiling. Gage gave a nod and stalked over to Terryn. She looked up at him with eyes wide enough to swallow her whole face. He dipped his head and kissed her full, deep and long. She was sagging in his arms by the time he ended it.

"Lower your eyes now, sub, and don't lift them again until you're given permission." Brice heard the edge in Gages voice, the tone that let him know his friend was entering his Dom state of mind and the playful gentleman façade was gone.

As Brice watched Gage lower the spreader bar to the floor in front of Terryn, he became hyper aware of his body and the desire thrumming through it. Gage wrapped the ankle cuffs around first one delicate ankle and then ordered her to widen her stance until she was lined up for the next. After Gage attached the second one, Brice heard his hum of appreciation.

"Oh you sweet thang," he rumbled, "I do love a nice pair of legs in shackles."

His large hands checked the fit of the cuffs to make sure they were snug enough but not in danger of pinching. Then those hands stroked and caressed their way up her mile-long legs. Brice could see Terryn quiver even from where he stood.

When Gage leaned forward and set his mouth on one of her sensitive inner thighs, Terryn's whole body jolted in reaction. As he bit and suckled up the length of that leg, she gasped and dug her hands in his hair. Brice could have warned her—he knew what was coming—but he was eager for what would come as a result, so he just settled back and watched the show.

"Little sub," Gage said as he locked an iron grip around her wrists. "Did I give you permission to touch me?"

Terryn jolted in shock at the question and then looked at him with wide eyes.

"And now you done gone and made it worse." He shook his head as he sat back on his knees. "Didn't I just tell you to keep your pretty eyes down until you were told you could lift 'em?" Too late, Terryn lowered her eyes and mumbled an apology but Gage was already set on a path. "If Brice had trained you better, we wouldn't be needin' to do this, so you can just lay what happens next at his feet. Now sit down and give me your hands."

Brice walked over to help her down since her legs were shackled. Once she was seated, he leaned her forward and guided her hands to clasp the middle of the bar.

Gage grabbed the wrist cuffs and clasped them in place. He ordered, "Even with the cuffs, I want you to hold on tight." Then Brice stepped back and reached for the switch that would raise the bar.

As Terryn was lifted slowly into the air, Gage riffled through the duffle he'd gotten from his locker. He pulled out a riding crop that Brice was fond of. It was slender and made of a nicely flexible fiberglass stem with a soft leather flap. Terryn hadn't seen it yet since all her focus was on herself at the moment. She was completely off the floor now and as the bar lifted higher and higher she began to pant and whimper.

Since Gage was taller and currently had the lead, Brice kept her going until her ass was at a perfect level for him. Once it stopped, Terryn hung there swaying and panting while he and Gage enjoyed the view. Her legs spread wide and clamped tight with her arms secured to the center of the bar. Long red hair shrouded her shoulders and the upper curve of her back while that delectable ass was wide open and exposed—just waiting for whatever they wanted to do to it.

Terryn gripped the bar so tight her knuckles turned white. She was spread wide, folded in half and hanging, ass in the air in a room with two fully clothed men. When she'd dreamed about this lifestyle, she hadn't even come close to a situation like *this*.

Gage hummed his approval of the picture she made and ran one large hand along the "V" of her legs, leaving goose bumps in his wake. Brice stepped up behind her and grasped a handful of her hair and used it to tilt her head back and take her lips.

His kiss was not what she had been expecting. She'd braced for a brutal plunder of her mouth and instead what she got was a tender, sweet seduction. He nipped at her lips and laid feather-light brushes of his tongue along each one until she was open and straining for him.

She wanted nothing more than his mouth sealed to hers and he denied her, pulling back and tightening his grip on her hair until she settled herself to take only what he gave. Then the warm scrape of Gage's work-roughened hand was replaced by a cool tickle and Terryn risked more punishment by lifting her eyes to see what Gage was doing.

"Oh God." It was a riding crop. Both men chuckled at her shocked whisper and then Brice stepped back and hit the remote for her breasts.

At first Gage just stroked the crop lightly along the same path that he'd taken with his hand. Next, he didn't really hit her—it was more like a fluttering up and down her thighs and across her bottom. Then he shocked a gasp from her with a firm smack on the sole of both her feet in fast succession. While her toes curled and she pulled at her arms with no result, she got her first sharp snap from the crop. It landed right in the center of her left butt cheek and Terryn was more surprised than stung. He wasted no time in landing the next on her right cheek. Then more up and down her legs again, some soft as a kiss, others harsh as the sting of a wasp.

The whole time, the pads on her breasts were in constant use, sucking and vibrating with differing speeds and force. The crop was never still and Gage didn't stick to a pattern so she could do nothing to brace herself for the sharper slaps of it. The warming sensation started as a tickle on the soles of her feet which he kept coming back to with quick stings from the crop, and it grew in intensity as it got closer to her bottom. All that intensity was pulsing toward her core.

Terryn felt herself drifting and her vision turned white at the edges. She started losing her focus—she couldn't remember where Brice was standing and she kept forgetting that her arms were immovable. Every time she received a sharp smack, she tried to let loose so she could shield her bottom. She didn't know if she was more turned on or frustrated by her restraints. That warming turned into a low-level burn in her ass and it was seeping up into her pussy to set fire to her entire lower half.

She shook her head, thinking that might somehow clear it and help her focus. Then—*CRACK*—the first hit that she would call a whipping landed right in the center of one cheek and Terryn let out a shout. *CRACK*. Again he did it, and again.

Just when she felt like she was going to cry, he stopped and that big strong hand was exploring her throbbing flesh. He murmured, "Poor baby," and then the pad over her clit hummed to life.

"She's got a sweet little cunt on her, Gage." Brice's voice seemed to float over the room from nowhere. "Taste her."

Her brain was foggy, but Terryn had enough working cells to blush over that, then Gage replied, "Mmm, is that so?" and lowered his head.

The crop hung from his wrist while his hands held her lips open and his tongue delved inside. She couldn't hear his moan over her own breathless cry—but she felt it. It reverberated through every inch of her body as he suckled and lapped while his blunt fingers tugged on her lips with just enough force to add another layer of sensation. She didn't know that the keening she heard was from her own mouth until Brice whispered, "Shhhh, easy," and ran a comforting hand down her side.

Gage lifted his head and told Brice, "Damn, son, I think you're right."

Then he started with the crop again. Hard, soft, all the way up to her knees and back down again. When the tingle of each individual slap morphed into a constant, relentless burn, he stepped back and slapped that crop right onto her swollen and pulsing sheath. Her scream echoed in the room as her whole body locked and swayed in her restraints.

She hadn't come, but it was like hanging on the edge of a climax—a climax that had teeth. Her vision went white and there was a buzzing in her ears as every part of her reached for the release that would set her free. She felt drunk and energized at the same time. Terryn couldn't think beyond one simple word: *Please. Please, please, please.* It echoed through her brain like a chant, only she couldn't have said whether she was begging for them to stop or for them to go on forever.

She heard them talking from what seemed like miles away. Although she couldn't make out everything they were saying, some disjointed words seeped through the fog in her brain. Phrases like "sub-space" and "never d.p.'d" and "plug out" were some of them. She couldn't make sense of them and didn't think she even wanted to try. All she could do was hang there in an agony of suspense while the men with the power to end that suspense decided what they were going to do to her.

Brice startled her when he slung what looked like a very wide belt along her back. He kissed her temple and shushed her as he adjusted it to his liking and checked its connection to a ceiling hook. Then he unfastened her cuffs from the bar and eased her back into the belt, shifting it and her as she was slowly stretched out. When he was satisfied, her wrists were now cuffed to the belt, her shoulders and head were lower than her hips and her legs were still suspended in a "V" from the bar. It was strange to be essentially lying down in midair and the feeling of floating was heightened by the arousal still throbbing through her blood.

She was looking over her body and adjusting to this new position when Gage stepped into her view between her widespread legs. Her eyes locked on his now-bare chest and lower as she watched him roll a condom onto his enormous erection and Terryn's already foggy brain went foggier. The body that had been teasing her on the dance floor was even better than she had imagined. She wasn't a bodybuilding expert, but she was sure *he* had to be. Muscles bulged and defined every inch of him and Terryn heard herself gulp. Loudly.

He reached between her throbbing cheeks. "Hang on, sugar," he told her in his honey-rich drawl. "I'm takin' this out before we get started."

At first she couldn't think what he meant, and then he grasped the plug. He didn't just remove it—instead, he played with it first. He nudged it in deeper with tiny pulses, then he made circles with it while the pad over her clit came to life again. She was already so close to the edge she was sure it was going to send her over, but just as those first waves crested, he pulled the plug out and left her gasping.

Brice cupped a gentle hand on her face and turned her toward him. "Open up, baby. Let me in."

The velvety head of his cock teased her lips and as she allowed him to slide deep inside, Gage entered her from below in one slow, sure push. He felt so different than Brice—he was thicker and as he continued his forward glide, he seemed longer too. Which was worrisome enough to chase back a little of the fog from her mind. Brice was not a small or even moderate-sized man and she worried that Gage might be more than she could take. Terryn shuddered when he finally reached the end of himself. Or maybe it was the end of her; she couldn't tell and didn't care. All she knew was she felt invaded and full and completely taken over. Her ass was still tingling from the plug. The nerves there throbbed and pulsed from the stretching and pressure of having Gage inside her.

The men waited for her to adjust. She wouldn't say they were still. There was too much power in their bodies to call all that coiled tension stillness. To Terryn, it closely resembled the way a jungle cat stalks, muscles bunched and quivering in anticipation of the perfect moment to pounce and devour its prey. When her eyes lifted and met Brice's, the look on his face only intensified that image in her mind. An adrenaline rush of fear mixed like a heady wine with her arousal until she felt her whole body shudder in reaction. As if that were the signal they had been awaiting, they both moved as one.

Gage slid his hands along her legs until he had a firm grip on her thighs, anchoring her to him, and Brice grabbed what she was coming to think of as his favorite handle—a fistful of hair. Then they began thrusting and rocketed Terryn into heaven. She'd never dreamed that having two men at once would be like this. She hung suspended between them, wholly at their mercy as they tunneled in and out of her body while all she could do was take it.

Gage moved his grip from her thighs to her butt cheeks and squeezed, once, twice, three times with hard jolting thrusts and he chuckled as her body exploded on cue in an orgasm that had her gurgling a scream around Brice's shaft. He said something to Brice and then before she had a chance to catch her breath, one thick finger thrust into her ass while the clit pad went turbo and Terryn's world went black then white as she was catapulted back into orbit again. Ricochets of pleasure bombarded her when the incredible pulses centered in her core.

Brice had eased out from her mouth for that one and as she panted and gasped in the aftermath, he slid back between her lips. Terryn sucked him back in with everything she had and was rewarded by his dark hiss and the telling quiver in his legs. With one last pump, Gage slipped his finger from her ass and returned his grip to her thighs. She heard the deep rumble of them as they spoke to each other again. Too far gone to know what was said, Terryn sensed a new force to their lovemaking. Suddenly, she could tell they had decided that playtime was over and they were about to get serious.

It lasted forever. It was over too soon. She thought she was done climaxing. If asked, she would have said it would be impossible for her to come again after the force of the ones she'd already had. Then the pads on her nipples and her clit blazed to sudden, brutal life and she was powerless against it. Terryn was unable to even arch within the tight grips of the men when her body simply locked as the force of the next orgasm set every bone on fire until she was nothing but living flame between them.

Gage started losing his rhythm next. His griped turned viselike on her thighs and he pulled her into his increasingly harder thrusts with deep, growling grunts. Terryn felt him swell to an unbelievable size seconds before he roared and she felt the heat and throb of his release through his condom while he pounded into her to the end.

Brice pulled her focus back to him then when he shoved farther into her mouth than he ever had before, tilting her head back at an angle that allowed him to deep throat her. She watched his face as he watched his shaft plunge between her lips over and over. Within moments, his lips curled back in a snarl. As deep as he was, she couldn't do anything but take as he roared and that first bitter, hot splash bathed her mouth.

It was some minutes before either of them could move. Terryn was profoundly grateful that she was supported and equally glad that as the sub, aftercare was up to someone else.

Nothing in her life had ever been like that. A burning sensation was starting to penetrate her senses as the fog slowly lifted from her brain. The backs of her thighs and especially the cheeks of her ass felt like she had a good sunburn going on. There was also serious doubt in her mind that she'd ever walk or sit down again. She sighed and thought that was just fine with her.

Chapter Thirteen

At the Surf-N-Slurp, Angie was closing up for the night. The espresso machine was clean. The tables were washed and the counters wiped down. She had tomorrow's breads and muffins already mixed and waiting for the oven first thing in the morning. She stopped at the back door with the trash—her last duty of the day—waiting at her feet.

She looked over the shop like she always did, making a final visual sweep of the place just to be sure she caught everything. Assured that all was as it should be, she dragged the garbage bag out the back door with her. She was ticking each step off the list she needed to follow to get ready for her late-night date.

"First, stuff this stinkin' mess in the stinkin' dumpster." She huffed as she dragged the heavy black bag closer to its final resting place. "Second, go make a final sweep for lowlifes hidin' in the bathrooms, then hit the lights and hurry, so I don't miss the train home again and stinkin' have to wait a half hour for stinkin' nothin'."

With a mighty heave, she flung the bag up and into the overflowing bin then she cursed fluently when the landing caused a revolting spray of coffee grounds to splatter her arms and face.

"Eww! Yuck." Angie frantically wiped at her eyes and spit out grounds in between profanities. "Son of a—"

She never saw the bat coming. One bright startling flash of pain and then it was over. As her body crumpled to the ground, she didn't feel the repeated hits that fractured her skull nor the ones that broke her bones as the blows continued to rain down with merciless glee. She most certainly didn't hear the laughter.

Brice was feeling pretty freaking smug. He looked over at the woman curled up in the seat next to him and it took quite a bit of self-control to keep from gloating. Terryn was back in her little black dress, minus the belt and its accessories, and looked about as substantial as steam. She kept glancing at him with stars in her eyes and making a sound that was a cross between a sigh and a hum. It made him feel like Superman.

His eyes locked with Gage's over her head and the two shared a moment of silent accord. They both were experienced enough to know that what had happened tonight with Terryn was rare. It had been like a perfectly choreographed dance with one hell of a crescendo. Brice watched what could only be called a shit-eating grin spread across Gage's face and felt an identical one on his own. He looked down at Terryn and the grin just got bigger. She was the sub he'd been searching for since that very first night back in college. He knew it was fast, but he also knew that with each new discovery into who she was, he only fell deeper.

"Hey." He nudged her shoulder. "You want to stop at the Surf-N-Slurp for some late-night coffee? They stay open late, don't they?"

Terryn looked up with sleepy eyes. "Yeah, if we aren't going straight to sleep when we get to your place, I'll need coffee." Her smile was all sexy, satisfied woman and damn if it didn't make him want to satisfy her again. He looked up and got a nod from Gage, then gave the new direction to the cabbie.

As Brice helped Terryn from the cab, Gage paid the fare and they headed for the door. Locked. Terryn made a sad sound and pointed out that they missed it by ten minutes.

"Why are the lights still on, though?" she asked.

Brice felt a sick twist in his gut. "Gage, hold on to her here for a minute," he said. When Terryn reached for his hand and started to speak, Brice just shook his head. "Stay here with Gage and I'll be right back."

Brice didn't tell her it was nothing. He was rarely off when his instincts were firing like they were now, so he didn't bother to give her a false line about him probably being paranoid. He just left them frowning after him as he pulled his gun and headed for the back entrance.

"Sonofagoddamnfuckingbitch!"

Angie. It was Angie lying in a pool of blood next to the garbage.

He wanted to rush to her and hold her, but the training and years as a cop choked that first gut urge and made him sweep the alley for any signs of the perp. His eyes scanned everything around her. The door to the coffee shop was shut and there were no cars in sight.

He fished his phone out of his pocket and spoke into it without putting his gun away or taking his eyes off the alley. As he moved in to check for a pulse, he did it with a heavy heart, sure that there would be none. First dial was to dispatch to call it in, then he hit his partner's number. As the thing rang once then once more, he felt the fury and anguish boil up inside him like a pressure cooker. He didn't have a clue what he was going to say to Kent when a miracle happened.

Angie moved her arm.

"Brice," he dimly heard, "You know I got a date—"

"Surf-N-Slurp! Fucking now!" he shouted. He was loud enough that he heard Gage and Terryn call out and come running. Then he hung up and called 9-1-1 as he rushed to her side. Just as the operator picked up, Terryn and Gage rounded the corner. The big Texan cursed loud and long while Terryn let loose with a moan of denial even as she knelt down and reached to help. Brice gave the address and handed the phone off to Gage. Then he told Terryn, "We need to try and stop the bleeding. Put pressure there and just hold on." He motioned toward Angie's side where blood was welling in a gruesome puddle beneath her.

"She's alive," she said with a sob. "Oh thank you, God, she's alive." When Angie gave a weak moan and tried to sit up, Brice would have stilled her but Terryn beat him to it. "Shh, don't move, Angie. You poor thing, you have to keep still."

Brice reached out as gently as he could and braced his hands on Angie's neck in the hopes of stabilizing it. The amount of damage she was showing, there was a better than good chance that she had a spinal injury. The important thing was to keep her from exacerbating it before the paramedics got here with a brace. Gage prowled back and forth behind them while Terryn tried to put pressure on the wound that looked the worst. And the whole time Brice held her neck he prayed that his partner would get here fast.

When Kent's car screamed up to the alleyway ten minutes later, Brice was there to intercept as he leaped from behind the wheel. The blue and red lights of the ambulance flashed over his grief-ravaged face. He tried to barrel past him to get to the scene, but Brice grabbed his arms.

"She's alive," Brice said. It didn't register; Kent kept shoving to get by. With grim resolve, he held fast and shouted into his friend's face, "Kent, she's alive!" When some of the wildness leached away from those eyes and focused on him, he repeated, "She's alive. It's bad, buddy. The son of a bitch beat her, but she's alive. The medics are loading her up now, so you go see her, but I had to warn you, it's bad."

Brice stepped back and watched Kent gather himself before rushing to the gurney. Even with the warning, Brice heard his anguished cry as Kent got a look at what had been done to her. His shaking hands hovered over the bandage obscuring most of her face, clearly afraid to touch her and cause more pain. Then he settled for fisting his hands in the sheet of the gurney. He was murmuring to her in a voice too low for Brice to hear and the sight broke his fucking heart. He wasn't the least surprised when Kent loaded into the ambulance with the gurney, nor was he surprised by the aggression when he put a restraining hand on Kent's arm.

"Easy, partner," Brice said, clear and calm. "I'm not trying to stop you, I just need your keys." Kent stared at him blankly for a moment before the words registered, then he nodded and handed them over, "I'll have your car at the hospital in the morning. I'll finish up here and see you tomorrow."

As the ambulance pulled away, Brice locked down the side of himself that wanted to weep. He locked away the anger and the sadness, he locked everything away but the cop. Then he turned back to his crime scene and determined that he wasn't leaving this alley until it told him everything.

"Where's her purse?" Terryn's sleepy voice came from the depths of Kent's backseat. Brice had just started the car to

135

leave, but her question gave him pause. "Don't you think we should grab her coat and purse for her? Or did you have to tag it or something for evidence?"

Brice twisted around to look at her. She was snuggled under Gage's coat with her head resting in his lap. Both of them looked bleary-eyed and tired, but neither of them had uttered a word of complaint and they had refused to leave without him.

"Her purse wasn't in the alley," he answered. His sluggish mind knew that that was significant for some reason and he was struggling to figure out why. "It was still in the shop."

"Hmm," Terryn said, "weird."

"Weird, why?" he asked.

"Because," she answered with a yawn, "if she wasn't leaving for the night, why was the door locked?"

"The door was locked?" Brice tried but couldn't remember trying to get in himself until the place was already flooded with cops and Jenny the owner was there answering questions and serving them all coffee.

"Mm-hmm," came her sleepy reply. "I wanted to wait in there after they took Angie, but it was locked. Jenny had to come and let everyone in." Then her eyes drifted shut and she was out. Brice, however, was wide-awake again. Adrenalin fired through his system while he mentally reviewed the facts.

The lights had still been on and the open sign had been flashing its cheery welcome when they'd pulled up in the cab.

Angie's purse, jacket, cell phone and keys had all still been in the back room.

The door had been locked.

The lock was a two-way dead bolt.

Brice held the door to his apartment open so Gage could carry Terryn in. She looked delicate in the arms of the big Texan. Her hair was a fiery cloud around her face and obscured all but one pale cheek. Gage, having been a frequent guest, headed straight for the bedroom without asking for directions or needing a light. Brice beat him there and tugged the blankets back so he could lay her between the sheets.

With a low murmur, Gage set her down and gently slid her dress from her. Brice stepped into the bathroom and came back with a damp cloth just as Gage was stretching out beside her. He first ran it over her face, wiping away the remains of her makeup and the grime from the alley. He washed her neck, arms and hands next. She cooed like a dove when he came back with a second cloth and proceeded to bathe her breasts. Not one to be left out, Gage helped by draping one of her thighs over his hips so Brice had easy access to cleaning between them. They'd all thoroughly cleaned up before leaving the club earlier, so this was more to pamper her than anything else. She was soft and pink and perfect down there. He could happily spend the rest of his life exploring her.

When Gage shifted to pull the covers over them, Terryn's whisper stopped them both. "I just want to forget. It hurts so bad, and I'm so scared for Angie and I can't get it out of my head. Please, make me forget." Her eyes were tear-drenched and Brice heard Gage swear under his breath when she looked at him as well. "Please. Just make it all go away." Brice's fingers gentled even more and he let the washcloth slip from his hand.

She was growing warm and wet. Those pale-as-cream cheeks flushed with color and her luscious lips parted as her breathing increased. Brice watched as Gage slid a hand over her ribs to cup and fondle one full breast. When those fingers plucked and pinched at her nipple he felt the first stirrings of urgency in his blood.

Brice slid his touch to her back entrance and circled there. He leaned forward and swirled his tongue around her glistening clit, waiting until she arched and moaned, then slid his longest finger—slow and sure—into that tight ring.

Her cry of pleasure was music to his ears. With his eyes closed, he enjoyed the symphony of soft sighs and low groans as he and Gage let their hands and mouths explore the body she so generously offered. When next he opened his eyes, he had two fingers buried in each of her holes and her clit suckled deep against his tongue. Gage had shifted to kneel beside her and his cock was stretching her pretty mouth wide.

Terryn's clit swelled and her body went suddenly rigid, but Brice pulled back just in time. "Not yet, sub." His voice was gravel-deep with his own arousal. "Not just yet, baby." She whimpered sexily as he shoved her knees to her to her armpits and crossed her ankles over her chest. "Hold them there," he told her and guided her hands to clasp her feet. "Stay just like that and don't let go." She was spread wide and her hips were tilted at just the right angle for what he had in mind.

"Nice." Gage looked away from her face to see how he'd positioned her and smiled his approval.

Brice reached over to the bedside drawer for necessities and covered himself, then grabbed a tube of lubricant. He felt Terryn jerk when he squirted the cold gel on to her, but she didn't let go and continued to wring grunts and moans out of Gage. With a murmured "Good girl," he kept going.

He brought his knees up close so she was cradled between them and slowly, so slowly eased his cock into her snug back hole. The ring of taut muscles there reflexively clenched and then gave under the pressure. After what felt like an eternity to him, he was in as far as he could go. Terryn froze and tried to let go of her legs. Brice grabbed her wrists and held. It was another agony of waiting, but he gave her time to adjust.

Gage muttered a few choice words about how good his view was and even as he continued to plunge in and out of her mouth, he reached down and rubbed three blunt fingers over her dripping wet sheath. The added stimulation helped to ease her into this first taking of her ass.

Brice watched as he slid his fingers inside her and then pulled them out to massage her clit, only to plunge back in again. All the while, Brice kept working his shaft in small pulses till at last he felt her body relax and yield to his Will. She was tight and hot and perfect.

"Sweet God in heaven," he rasped.

Slowly he started to thrust. Her ass surrounded him like nothing he'd ever felt and as the indescribable pleasure increased so did his rhythm, until he was pounding into her. His hands gripped like iron bands around her wrists. The more he gave her, the more frantic she became. They had her securely restrained—her only option for movement was her mouth on Gage's cock and she poured all her passion out there. Her muffled cries blended with the wet sounds of sex as she sucked and lapped at him, reducing the big man to a trembling mountain beside her.

Gage roared as he started to come and pumped his fingers inside her sheath with renewed vigor. He plunged them fast and hard up against her g-spot and with a scream she joined him in climax, her juices splashing out around his hand while his filled her mouth.

It was too much for Brice's system to take. Her already tight ass locked on to him and he was powerless to stop the avalanche that was his own climax. It was brutal and unstoppable and Brice felt a pleasure so intense it bordered on pain as it barreled its way through his body and poured into hers.

He collapsed forward and the three of them panted and floated in the aftermath. With a few twitches and aftershocks, he pulled out from Terryn and reached for one of the washcloths from earlier. He smiled at her as he brought it up to wipe her face while Gage grabbed one and ran it gently between her legs.

"Maybe we should let you do this," he told her and kissed the tip of her nose. "If we start this again, we may never get to sleep."

"Fine by me," Gage rumbled, his voice not yet recovered. "Damn fine sub you got here, Brice." Then he lobbed the washcloth toward the bathroom and snuggled up to Terryn's back with a happy sigh. Brice settled into place at her front and with a few adjustments they were set.

"I know, Gage," Brice replied, "I know."

She smiled up at him with sleepy eyes and he couldn't help but to lean in for a long, tender kiss. She was the perfect sub for him. Generous and sweet and so open to everything he taught her. She was also smart and kindhearted. In the brief time he'd known her, she had shown him depths of strength and courage that left him humbled and depths of passion that left him breathless. As sleep pulled him down, a single conviction took hold of his heart.

"I'm never letting you go," he whispered it as both their eyes drifted shut, "Never."

Chapter Fourteen

Terryn let herself into her apartment and stumbled to the couch. Once she got there, though, she didn't know what to do. Every muscle in her body ached and her butt felt like it was sunburned thanks to her first lesson in erotic spankings. Since she was alone and there was no one there to think less of her for it, she let out a whine. She wanted nothing more at this moment than to plop down and rest, but she couldn't think how to do that when there wasn't a part of her that wasn't sore and tender.

When her cell went off, she allowed herself one more whine and answered it with a smile in her voice if not on her face. "Hello."

"I thought you had today off," Brice's voice crooned in her ear and Terryn flushed at just the sound of him. *Jeez*, she thought, *I'm pathetic.* "I called you at my place and Gage said you went to work."

"I did have it off, but they needed me so I went in for a partial shift this afternoon." Her legs felt like rubber, so she gave up waiting for a miracle and eased down to the cushions. *Yep. That hurts.*

"Terryn?" The note of concern in Brice's voice was unmistakable. "What's wrong? Are you hurt?"

"No, not really." She shifted a little and tried to ease over onto one hip. Nope. Not helping. "Just feeling a little tender and sore from last night." As hard as she tried to not to, a squeak escaped when she tried the other hip. The warm and fuzzy feelings she was harboring for Brice dropped to freezing when his chuckle hit her ear.

"Next time I should beat on you and see if you aren't the one who's sore. And then maybe I'll stick something up your butt too. See how you like that." His laughter was as infuriating as it was comforting and didn't that just confuse the heck out of her?

"It doesn't work like that, Red," he said with the laughter still rich and warm in his voice. "Unfair, I know, but nothing we can do about it." He paused for a second and then asked, "Why did you go to your place and not mine? I thought the plan was to spend the weekend together."

"Well," Terryn said as she gave up trying to be brave and whimpered when she stretched out on the couch. "It was the plan. Then you had to get up early and work and I got called into work too, so I thought the plan was a bust." She stopped herself from saying what the biggest reason for her being back at her place was.

"And Gage being at my place didn't have anything to do with that, did it?" Terryn should have known he'd zero in on that. He was so good at reading her it didn't even surprise her that he'd guessed. "Talk to me, Terryn. How much did Gage have to do with your decision to go back to your place?"

"A lot." She gave in with a sigh. "I don't know. I really like him. He's so sexy and strong and God, is he ever good in bed."

"Terryn," Brice interrupted with a new edge to his voice, "don't make me kill my best friend."

She giggled. "Sorry. But he's wonderful. I really like him. Only—he's not you. And I don't know, I guess I felt wrong somehow being there when you weren't. Like, like—it sounds dumb—but it's like without you there it's almost like I'd be cheating or something." She waited for a while and when he didn't say anything she asked, "Is that stupid? Am I being stupid?"

"No, Red." His voice was soft and she was back to warm fuzzies when he said, "Not at all. In fact, I'm sorry I didn't think of that myself so you wouldn't be home alone and feeling awkward. You were there as my sub, so it's natural that you would feel that way left alone with another Dom. You knew that even though I was okay with him joining us and touching you with my permission, without me there it would feel wrong." He paused for a minute. "Do you know why that is, sub?"

"No, Sir," Terryn answered, feeling a tingle of awareness in response to his Dom voice.

"It's because you belong to me and even though we haven't talked about commitments or arrangements, your body knows it." Another long pause. "And, Terryn? So does mine."

Brice hung up his cell and allowed himself one more moment of gloating. What he had with Terryn felt solid and right and good. He'd had no interest in a permanent relationship before meeting her. Now the thought of not having her with him permanently caused a disturbing amount of panic in his gut.

After this case was closed, they'd have that talk about commitments and arrangements. They'd have to make some adjustments on both sides. He'd insist on her moving in. That was a hard line for him. Although her neighborhood was nice enough, he wanted her in his arms every night. On his end, he was going to have to find a way to pull back at work without letting his cases suffer. There were plenty of guys on the force who had found the right balance. No reason to think he couldn't also.

With his mind settled on the next phase of his life with Terryn, he switched gears and turned to look into the coffee shop he had been sitting in front of while they'd talked. *See*, he silently told himself, *compartmentalizing already*. Then he got out of the car and headed in to talk to the owner.

"Hello, Detective." Jeannette Hankins looked up at him with a grief-ravaged face and didn't bother trying to force a smile.

She was an attractive woman in her late thirties with chin-length brown hair and round hazel eyes. She was smart and had a sense of humor that she used with charming skill on everyone who crossed her path. Including him. He'd let her tease and charm him, both he and his partner had, and now two of her employees were dead while a third one barely clung to life. He'd never even considered her. Had he let a killer deceive him? He was here to find out.

"Hi, Jenny." She noticed something in the way he spoke because her hands stilled and her eyes filled. "Oh, God." He watched what color she had drain from her face. "She's gone? Is Angie gone?" Brice quelled the urge to comfort, trying to see a killer in what he'd previously decided was an innocent woman.

"No, Jen, no. Angie is still in ICU—there's no change." When she wilted in relief, Brice asked, "Where were you last night?"

She looked at him in puzzlement. "I was here as soon as I got the call from one of your officers. I let you all in and made everyone coffee."

"Where were you when you got the call?"

"I was home with Bill and the kids. Before that we were at a ball game. Bill coaches for our youngest and we all go to help out at the concession stand." She crossed her arms over herself in a protective gesture. "Am I a suspect, Detective?"

"I'm asking the whereabouts of everyone connected. What time was the game over?"

Brice watched her eyes dart around the room. "Nine o'clock."

"Late for a Little League game, wasn't it?"

She bit her lip and answered, "Not really. It got over earlier than that, but we had to help out. You know, close out the stand and clean up and stuff." She tugged at one ear and then scratched at her neck. She was awful fidgety for a mom recounting her kid's Little League game.

"Care to tell me why you're so nervous?" He pointed to her hand that was now scratching at her leg and she visibly forced herself to relax.

"It's just..." A huge sob broke from her chest. "Just that I'm scared. I'm scared that my shop is going to close down because no one is coming here for coffee anymore and—and—and what if he comes after me next?"

She crumpled. Brice watched in horror as she simply dropped out of view and disappeared behind the counter. He heard her sobbing voice float up from the floor. "I'm next, I know it and I got kids and my husband and I don't wanna lose my shop and I'm scared and what am I going to do?"

With all the caution he would use approaching a bomb, Brice leaned over the counter and looked down. She was hunched over with her arms clasped around her middle, sitting cross-legged. She rocked back and forth and continued to sob out her misery to the floor. "I'm a terrible person. I should be

145

worried about my poor girls. Katie and Amber and now poor sweet Angie but all I can think about is me and my stupid business. I'm awful. I-I-I-I'm a bad person." Then the rest was lost in some pretty impressive wailing.

The bell above the door chimed. Brice looked over to watch the customer who came in pause and go wide-eyed at the sound of weeping. She looked at Brice and he just shrugged and pointed over the counter to where Jenny continued to bawl.

"Maybe you should come back later," he told her even as she turned and fled. He walked back to the door and locked it behind her. When he came back, Jenny was pulling herself up with both hands and looked like she'd aged about twenty years in the last ten minutes.

"I don't even know why I opened today. I should have stayed home. I should have. Bill told me to." She gave a watery huff. "Shit, Bill told me to close permanently and sell." She looked at him with her heart in her eyes. "I can't sell. I love this place. And, Detective, believe it or not, part of why I love this place is my girls. I do. I love my girls and I can't take this." She seemed to steel herself and then asked, "Are you arresting me?"

Brice grabbed a napkin from the counter and handed it to her. "No. I'm not arresting you." *Yet.* "Your back door is locked with a deadbolt."

She blew her nose and answered, "Yes."

"Any way for it to be locked without a key?"

Another blow and snuffle. "No."

"Can you explain how Angie was out in the alley with her keys inside and yet you had to come let everybody in?"

The blowing stopped and Jenny looked at him with fresh horror.

"Whoever attacked Angie locked up before they left. Seems the killer loves this shop too."

In the family waiting area of the hospital, Brice sat knee to knee with Kent and filled him in on his little talk with Jenny. "Mandy is the only other employee and therefore key we have left. I went back through the belongings of the first two and both of their keys are accounted for."

"So unless someone made a copy, we are down to two suspects." Kent was haggard and wrung-out, but now he also looked determined.

"That's a big unless, but yeah. That's my take too." He motioned with his chin to the ICU. "How is she? Any change?"

"No." Kent ran a hand through his hair in frustration. "They have her in a medically induced coma. They said it's supposed to give her time for the brain swelling to go down. But with that they have to have a machine breathing for her and they can't get an accurate reading of her brainwaves, so they have no idea if she's going to come out of this a vegetable or not. Doc said the damn bastard beat the shit out of her skull. They said it's a miracle she didn't die on impact because her whole skull is a fucking spider web of cracks."

His shoulders slumped and he dropped his head into his hands with a barely controlled sob. Brice reached out and squeezed his shoulder in comfort. "Her right elbow was shattered, collarbone too, and a couple ribs. They had to remove her spleen—it was demolished." Kent looked up and locked eyes with him. "I don't know what I'm gonna do if she doesn't make it. She has to fucking make it." With another compressed sob, he shoved to his feet and paced to the window.

Brice sat where he was and watched helplessly while his partner battled the grief and worry. He knew Kent had been seeing Angie since Katie's funeral and if he'd had any doubts before about how serious it was, seeing the shape he was in right now eradicated them. They'd been partners for years and he knew that Kent needed the space to pull himself together. Giving him his space didn't stop his heart from breaking for him, though, didn't even come close.

After several painful moments, Kent wiped an angry hand under his nose and said, "I can't leave here yet. Not this soon. Leave me the background files and I'll go over them again. You go home."

"I'll stay," Brice said with a frown. Did Kent honestly think he'd leave him like this?

"No, really." Kent sat back down and faced him again. "You've been working this all day. Go. I'm here and re-reading these will take my mind off some of the worry, if I'm lucky. I saw Gage last night at the scene. Go. Go spend time with your friend and get some sleep. I'm fine."

Brice just got up and walked to the coffee station on the back counter. "So, you want any coffee with your sugar or should I just bring you this?" He held the sugar container up and wagged it back and forth without looking back.

Kent pushed back to his feet and joined him. "I'll make my own." Brice shook his head in wonder—guy shouldn't have a tooth left in his head with all that sugar. "Thanks," Kent said, staring into his coffee as he stirred.

"We're partners," Brice said with a shrug. "Thick and thin, right?"

"Right." Then the two of them sat down with the files and got back to the hunt for a killer.

Chapter Fifteen

Stupid! Stupid! Stupid! Stupid bat! Why did I use a bat? How stupid. Now she's not dead, the stupid bitch is in the hospital and everyone is all worried and praying for her and hoping she'll pull through. Everyone is as stupid as the bat. Why do they even care? The world is without one more slut once she stops being stupid and dies. I can't believe she didn't just die. Bitch.

Terryn walked into the Surf-N-Slurp not knowing what to expect. She'd come on an impulse. She felt so bad for Jenny. None of this was her fault—some sicko was targeting the girls that worked here and Terryn just knew this was killing her.

Maybe she was crazy. Maybe she was taking a useless risk, but Katie had loved Jenny and loved this place and Terryn did too. Not to the same extent that Katie did, but enough that when Jenny looked up from behind the counter the first thing she said was, "So, can I get free coffee through my whole shift or am I limited to just one a day?"

"Huh?" Jenny looked like she hadn't slept for the last week. Her confusion and exhaustion were plain on her face.

"Coffee?" Terryn said as she stepped behind the counter and reached for one of the aprons hanging on the back wall. It was brown and had a slogan on it that read: "There's too much blood in my caffeine system." All the aprons were fun and came in a rainbow of colors with a different saying or picture on each one. It was a trademark of the Surf-N-Slurp and one of the things that made the café stand out. "I know the girls all get free coffee as a perk. What I wanna know is if I'm limited to one a day or is it a no-holds-barred kind of thing?"

"You want to come work here?" Jenny's hazel eyes filled and her bottom lip quivered. "That's so sweet. You would do that for me? Really?"

Terryn wrapped her in a hug. "Of course. Why wouldn't I?" Jenny let out a watery snort and gave her a look that comment deserved. "Well, maybe not of course. I'm not stupid. But Katie loved you and I love you and I honestly think a full third of the population of New York will die of caffeine withdrawal if you close down. I can't in good conscience let that happen. So I'm here to help."

"You sweet thing." Jenny cupped a hand on Terryn's face. Terryn had seen her do it dozens of times to her daughters and the girls who worked for her. "I love you for offering. But it's too dangerous. As much as I need you, I can't let you or anyone else take that kind of risk." She looked around at the deserted dining area with a watery sigh. "I can't just shut down, but I won't put anyone else in harm's way. I'll be working open to close and Bill will be dropping me off and then coming in to close with me every night. It'll be hard for a while, but I can't stand the thought of anyone else getting hurt."

Terryn looked at the circles under her eyes and said, "You'll have to teach me how to work the machine because I can barely make drip coffee that's drinkable. The baking will be cake, though." She smiled and gave Jenny a nudge to move her to the side so she could wash her hands in the small sink. "I have always been a wiz at baking."

Jenny shook her head and before she could add in more objections, Terryn barreled on. "It's only short term and only part-time. I work Monday through Friday at the center and I've arranged to cut back my hours so I can be here by four three days a week. I'll also work every other weekend for you —that way you can have some time with your family." She faced Jenny straight-on and looked her right in the eye. "We can't let him win. I know you are worried, but just like you have Bill, I'll have Brice." Terryn mentally crossed her fingers on this part because she was only hoping that he could come through. After all, she knew his work was highly unpredictable, so she would cross that bridge when she got to it. "I'll have him be here to close with me the way Bill will be here to close with you."

"I don't know, Terryn," Jenny hedged. "You are so sweet to offer, but I couldn't live with myself if you got hurt trying to help me."

"Look, Jenny," Terryn said, "I know there is risk. I know to be careful. The others didn't. I won't let my guard down and I am dating the detective who's going to put this psycho in a cage, so I think I'm pretty safe. Let me help."

Three and a half hours later, Terryn thought her feet were going to fall off. Right after her spine snapped in two. She was a quick study and had pretty much conquered the coffee-making part, so much so that Jenny had left her to mind the counter while she went back to the kitchen. Business was steady and even though she knew it was slow compared to what they normally did, it was more than enough to keep her on her toes.

She had just finished serving the last person in line when she heard the bell over the door chime. Mustering a smile, she looked up to greet more people and let go of her mini fantasy involving a break stretched out on the couch in the employee area. The smile froze when she saw who had just walked in.

Brice stood in the doorway looking confused for about thirty seconds. Then the confusion melted away and a murderous scowl darkened his handsome face.

Terryn upped the wattage on her smile and decided to brazen her way through. "Hey there, Detective. What can I get for you?"

"You can get your ass out from behind that counter, for one thing. For another, you can tell me just what in the hell you think you're doing." It was then that Terryn realized that maybe she should've mentioned to him what she had planned ahead of time.

"Jenny?" she called. "I need to take a quick break, if that's all right." Jenny hollered back that that was fine, so Terryn calmly stepped out from behind the counter and motioned for Brice to follow her to the break area in back. As soon as the door closed, she turned to face him.

"Look," she began, "I didn't plan this out very well. Looking at your expression right now, I'm thinking maybe I should have discussed my plans with you before I put this in motion."

She ignored his, "Damn right you should have," and kept talking.

"Jenny needs help. With what's happened, there's no way she's going to get anyone in here to work until that psycho is caught. Jenny is going to make herself sick trying to work this place with only Mandy to help." She reached out and laid a hand on his chest. "I have to help her. I have to. For Katie."

Brice layered his hand over hers and said in a soft and dangerous voice, "Over my dead body." Terryn gasped and tried to pull back, but he tightened his grip and she got nowhere. "This isn't a game and this isn't a movie. It's real live life and death going on here." His grip tightened more and he said, "Katie is dead, Terryn. Dead. Amber too and Angie is in a coma with a skull that looks like a piñata after Cinco de Mayo. You know what those poor girls had in common? Working here. That's it. That's the tie and there is nothing you say that's going to make me okay with you working here and putting yourself next in line."

Her gasp was loud and filled with temper. "You don't know that. You don't know for certain that is the only thing linking them together. And I know there's a risk. But you can't stop me from working here, Brice, you can't."

"Try me, Red." He gave her a look that promised she would be sorry if she did, but Terryn had already made up her mind. Even though she liked being bullied in the bedroom, she wasn't about to let him bully her out of it. "You think I won't close this place down? You think I can't? I can and I will if that's what it would take to keep you safe."

Terryn believed him. He wasn't just a highly respected detective—he was also from an extremely wealthy and well-connected family. Hell, at dinner he'd been chatting about the mayor and a bunch of other people who could easily follow through on his threat. He had a look in his eyes that convinced her he wasn't bluffing. She reached for patience and tried to focus on the fact that he was acting this way out of fear for her. It didn't change her mind or lessen her belief that she was doing the right thing, but it did help her remember to try and reason with him instead of fight. Fighting would just end up not only hurting them, but it could also close Jenny down.

"I thought about the risks. I was hoping you would help me there." She looked up at him and tried a small smile, thinking to herself that the old adage about bees and honey was a cliché for a reason. "I know that you work so hard already, but I was hoping that on the nights when I have to close you might be

153

able to see me home. You know, kinda like my very own bodyguard. That way I won't be scared and you will be here to make sure I'm safe."

She could see him think about it. She watched as he struggled to overcome his preference and consider what she wanted.

"I don't like it, Terryn. I don't like you anywhere near here until we catch this guy." His brows furrowed and he softened his grip on her hand while he brushed her hair from her cheek with his free hand. "Terryn, for me being a Dom isn't something that I turn on and off at will. It's in my blood—it's what makes me who I am. For some men, it's just a sexual preference and has nothing to do with the person they are on the inside. But for me and guys like Gage and my cousin, it's different. Deeper." He took a moment to kiss her forehead and tuck her head under his chin. Then she felt his arms come around her warm and secure while he said the rest.

"We're protective to a fault, overbearing, and in case you haven't noticed we like getting our way." He ignored her snort and continued, "I became a cop for a lot of reasons, but the underlying factor is that it serves the part of myself that needs to protect. Putting yourself in the crosshairs like this is going to shred every ounce of my focus. Because, Red, of all the people I want to protect, you've become the one that matters the most."

Terryn squeezed her eyes shut to keep tears back. His words were comforting and moving and made her hope for things with him that she was afraid to let take form in her heart. She couldn't let them sway her, though. She needed to stand strong and she needed him to be okay with that. It was more than helping Jenny now. Now it was also about him trusting her to make her own choices even when he didn't agree with them.

"I know we've only been seeing each other for like a second, but what I feel for you, Sir, is bigger and more real than anything I've felt with any other man. I want to be your sub. I want it in and out of the bedroom. There's a part of me that wants to sit up and say 'yes, Sir' to any and everything you ask of me." She paused for a moment and added, "That scares me to death. I need to know that being your sub doesn't mean I stop being me. You are the one with all the experience and I trust you to help me find the right balance here." She pulled back just enough to look him straight in the eye. "I need you to help me learn how to be your sub without losing who I am."

His eyes closed on a groan and those big strong hands that she loved so much slid up her arms and suddenly clutched around her neck. With a squeal of shock, she clasped on to his wrists just as he bent her over and started shaking her with mock growls.

She started laughing which only caused him to shake harder, and over her giggles she heard, "Why? Why did you have to put it that way?" Another couple of shakes and then he stopped to kiss her senseless. "I almost had you cowed. I could've gotten my way and kept you outta this, but you had to go and ask me to help you. Help you tell me no." He looked incredulous at that. "You actually got me to shut up and let you put yourself in danger then fixed it so you think I'm essentially doing something nice for you."

He shook his head, clearly baffled. "Fine. I want your schedule for the next two weeks. Here and for the rec center. Come hell or high water, I will be here every night you close."

She tried very hard not to gloat as she took out her schedule and copied it down for him and she even waited until he left before she did her happy dance.

"You gotta be fuckin' kidding me." Gage held a pool cue in one hand and beer in the other while he looked at Brice like he'd lost his mind. They were in the game room of Cade and Trevor's townhouse. The larger man hefted the cue like he was considering it as a weapon and Brice fleetingly hoped that his cousin had good homeowner's insurance.

Brice couldn't blame him—he felt like he must have lost his mind. Nothing else explained why he'd left Terryn in that damn coffee shop.

"You let her work there? Where the girls are gettin' killed?" Gage pointed his cue at him. "What the hell is wrong with you?"

Before Brice could offer an explanation, Trevor made his shot and said, "I'm wondering the same thing, man. When Terryn came into my office and asked me to cut back on her shifts, I thought it was because she wanted more time with you or that maybe she was still having trouble dealing with the loss of Katie. I did not know she was planning this. I don't think I would've agreed if I'd known."

Cade lined up his shot next and added, "Brice, I hate to gang up on you, but how in the hell did you let this happen?" The sharp crack of pool balls punctuated the question and Brice looked at three of the strongest Doms and best men he knew.

"She just might be it for me, guys. I think she's the one." If he thought his declaration was going to make them stop staring at him like he was crazy, he was mistaken. Now they looked even more convinced that he'd lost it.

"Which would make her working there even more inexplicable," Cade said.

With a groan, Brice lined up his shot and took it, not at all surprised to see it miss. He tossed down his cue on the table with a curse. "She's new to BDSM—you all know how new. I looked at her as we argued about this and I saw how desperately she wanted to please me. She is a sub down to her toes and she looked up at me all but quivering with the need to give me whatever I asked for." The men were no longer looking like they wanted to beat the crap out of him, so Brice took encouragement from that and went on.

"She also looked up at me and confessed that that was what she wanted. To please me in and out of the bedroom. Then she went and asked me to help her not lose who she was in the process of becoming my sub." He raised both hands in the air and then let them flop in frustration. "How in the hell could I say no after that? She said she trusted me to help her figure out how to be a sub without becoming a doormat." He snagged Gage's beer and downed half of it before asking them all, "What would you have done? When she put it that way, what else could I do but back off."

Trevor was the first to relent. One eyebrow quirked and he let out a soft curse as he racked up the balls to start another game. "Well, I'm glad I'm not you, man. That's all I can say." Brice picked up his stick and agreed with a grunt.

"Brice, my friend," Gage said as he took another beer from the mini fridge, "I hear what you're sayin' but she's still in danger. If I were you, I'd never let her work there. I'd chain her up in my room and keep her mind scrambled with a couple dozen orgasms a day until she forgot all about working there." He took a deep draw off his beer and grinned crookedly at them. "'Course, that's just me."

"Throw me another and come break," Brice said with a chuckle. "Jackass, you just wait till you meet yours. She'll tie you up in knots too. Just watch."

Gage handed him his beer and broke the balls with a satisfying crash and said, "No, sir, not me. For me it's gonna be a sweet li'l southern thang whose only goal in life will be to serve me."

Cade lined up his shot next and laughed outright. "Yeah, Gage, good luck with that."

Chapter Sixteen

The last customer of the evening left and Terryn locked the front door with a grateful sigh. As first days went, this one had been a doozy.

"Sweetie, why don't you head on out? Bill is here and I'll make him help me do the cleanup." Jenny's words were music to her ears.

Terryn thought that sounded like heaven, but she asked, "Are you sure? I don't want to run out on you if there is still a ton to do."

Jenny laughed and said, "Believe me, the cleanup stuff is easy and I got Bill here, so no worries. Go. The detective has been glowering in that booth for half an hour. You should put him out of his misery."

Terryn smiled, completely without remorse. Jenny didn't know it, but that glower was because he had plans for them tonight and every second longer it took just intensified the anticipation.

As soon as Terryn got in the waiting Town Car with Brice, he laid her back and clamped her hands over the arm rest. "Keep them there, sub, and don't speak a word until you are given permission."

Terryn nodded, her eyes wide at this stronger side of him. He looked dangerous and a little mean in the dim light. She had the thought that maybe this was his way of reclaiming his dominance since she'd gotten her way earlier. Whatever the cause, her body liked what he was doing and was already responding.

Brice set back in the seat and said, "Spread your legs." She did. "Wider." He picked up one and draped it over his lap while she moved the other out as far as she could and still be comfortable. "Now don't move."

She was wearing loose cotton slacks, so when Brice's hand slid up her thigh and settled on the soft folds of her sex she could feel the feather-light brushes of his fingertips without any difficulty. She bit lightly at her lip and looked at the privacy glass separating them from the driver. She'd never seen a Town Car with this feature before—it was just another glimpse of the luxury he had at his fingertips.

Terryn wondered if the driver could make out anything going on back here. She thought of what he'd see if he could. She was stretched out along three quarters of the seat with her arms over her head, her legs sprawled and Brice's hand playing between them as casual as you please. For a moment she wondered what it said about her that the thought of this unknown driver seeing this only added to the excitement.

Then Brice gave her another command and she stopped thinking about anything but what they were doing. "Pull your blouse up and unclasp your bra."

Her fingers trembled when she did it. His dark gaze zeroed in on her exposed breasts while his fingers kept up that maddening caress. It was too light now, too soft. She lifted her hips to show him she was ready for more pressure.

His reprimand was quick and sharp. Before she could guess his intent, he lifted his hand and brought it down with a snap that jolted from her core where he'd smacked her all the way to her fingertips and she stared at him in shock.

"Try a move like that again, Red, and you'll get more of the same." He didn't seem to be waiting for her consent, but she nodded her head anyway. Vigorously.

His fingers went back to teasing and he shifted a little, then leaned down and used his tongue, light and teasing, on her nipples. Terryn bit back a moan and watched helplessly while he lapped and sipped at her breasts. That dense, dark hair was too close-cut to fall forward on his forehead and she was thankful. Brice's breathtaking face was completely bare to her and she was as mesmerized by it as she was by what he was doing. Since his eyes were closed, she realized she'd never noticed how long and full those dark lashes were. He had a nose that was faultless in its symmetry and his cheeks had gone beyond five-o'clock shadow to outright stubble. His full lips were parted right now as that magic tongue flicked light as a dewdrop on her nipple. For this frozen moment in time, Terryn felt perfect.

"Absolutely perfect."

She didn't realize she'd said that aloud until Brice bit her. It wasn't a nip and it wasn't a tug. It was a bite and she yelped in surprise. The sadist chuckled and sucked the abused tip into his mouth to sooth the sting, then slanted a look up at her with an arched brow. Terryn bit her lips again, this time to keep from laughing and calling him a name that would only get her more punishment. She only hoped there wasn't too much traffic because if he was going to be dishing out torture like this all the way home she wasn't going to be able to keep quiet for long.

By the time the car pulled up to the building, Terryn was a mess. She was at such a point of arousal that she was sure she'd let Brice take her on the sidewalk if that's what he wanted. He sat her up to fix her bra and blouse himself.

"We aren't at your apartment, Terryn—we're at my cousin's place. Gage had to fly back to Texas, so the five of us are going to finish what we'd started the other night."

He didn't wait for her nod, but instead just opened the door and helped her out of the car. She barely noticed her surroundings as he led her through the club and into the playrooms. Everything around her was a swirl of pulsing colors and jagged need. When they stepped into the room where the others waited, Terryn stumbled to a stop and stared in fascination.

"Welcome to the wet room." Terryn gulped and Brice leaned close to whisper in her ear, "Strip."

The room was a giant shower. It looked sort of like the showers from high school but with extremely nice tile. It also had hoses and detachable showerheads everywhere. There were several restraint devices scattered about the room and a clear plastic tote against the wall. She could see it held a collection of toys that she didn't want to study too closely—she was better off not knowing what was coming. All of that, however, took a backseat to what was happening in the center of the room.

Riley was already naked, her slender arms stretched above her head and connected to a hook in the ceiling. Terryn had always been a little jealous of her curvy figure and now seeing her completely naked she knew she was right to be. The woman had a body that was full and lush and breasts that made Terryn sigh in envy. Riley was petite and, with her mixed heritage, she also had a perma-tan. Terryn knew she'd look like a skinny ghost next to her and suddenly she wasn't so eager to follow orders.

Brice stepped in front of her just then and when she raised her gaze to him his stern expression faded to gentleness. "Aw, Red." He lay a tender kiss on her lips. "You can't be thinking you have something to be shy about, can you?"

He tugged her slacks down her legs, not realizing or not heeding the fact that she was clutching to keep them on. "Riley is stunning, isn't she?" He looked over his shoulder to admire her as Trevor sprayed water on her back. Cade had another showerhead he'd set to strong pulses that he ran rhythmically over her breasts. "She's dark and curvy and beautiful." When he looked back at her, his smile was disarming. "Her beauty, Red, takes nothing from yours. You're tall and willowy where she's petite and rounded, and porcelain perfection where she's bronzed. And, you have noticed my preference for redheads, haven't you?"

Terryn smiled as she realized she was being stupid. Once out of high school, she'd never been one to suffer much from insecurities. So she let it go and looked back at where Riley was restrained. Anyone would've had second thoughts being compared to such a gorgeous woman, but she was over it now.

Naked, she stepped up to where Riley was getting thoroughly drenched by her two gorgeous men. Cade and Trevor were both shirtless and shoeless with Cade in black dress slacks and Trevor in low-slung blue jeans. They were in excellent, drool-worthy shape and Terryn felt a pang of envy for a whole different reason now.

Then she got to her spot and turned to face Brice. Every other thought faded. He stood in front of her, stripped of his shirt and shoes too. Her eyes followed the sleek musculature of his chest and abs. His black jeans hugged low so she could see the cut of muscle where hip met abdomen. The sight dried up her mouth and made her long to trace those ridges with her tongue.

"We're going to have a contest, Red," Brice told her just as Trevor stepped behind her and ran the warm water over her back. "Cade and Trevor are going to try and bring Riley to orgasm before I can bring you." He secured her hands above her head as he spoke. "Over and over again."

Terryn snuck a look at Riley and wondered how there could be a loser here. As Brice continued to talk, he reached into his pocket and pulled out two small rubber clamps that had slender chains attached to them. *Oh, that's how.*

"You will both be wearing nipple clamps that we will have rigged up with these water pails that Cade's setting up." With trepidation, she looked over at Cade, who had started threading thin rope from the plastic buckets through some sort of pulley thing in the ceiling. "Every time she beats you to a climax, you get water in your pail. The first one with a full pail loses."

Terryn gulped and looked toward Riley again. She thought if Riley's eyes got any wider they'd pop right out. It made her feel a little better that she wasn't the only one freaked out by this.

"Listen to me, sub. You don't want to let her beat you to even one, because as more water goes in, the harder it will be to reach the next orgasm." His voice was all rough and gravelly and she could see just how much he was looking forward to this in his face as well as the impressive bulge in those bad-boy black jeans.

He smiled like a pirate when she looked up from his crotch to meet his eyes and suddenly she was game. Terryn wanted to win. For him. She wanted him to win. She'd never played a sex game before and she was eager to embrace this first one with everything she had.

"Bring it." She gave him what she hoped was a cocky chin tilt and braced herself for a wet, wild night.

She absolutely blew his mind. There she stood, like an amazon. Proud and sure with her lovely body wet and flushed, her hair positively molten now that it was wet and her eyes all but glittering with the challenge.

He heard Cade chuckle at her bravado and looked over to see both him and Trevor admiring her. "You guys are going down."

"In your dreams," Trevor shot back. "We've spent the last two years learning every trick to bringing this sweet little one to peak. You, dude, are the one who's going down." Trevor said this as he was rubbing and squeezing Riley's shoulders like she was a prizefighter he was prepping for a fight.

"That may be true," Brice shot back. "But you forget. I've watched you all together and I happen to know that you have conditioned her to hold out and hold back. Whereas my sub is new to all of this and she gives up her climaxes like ripe fruit from a tree." Trevor looked taken aback at that and whipped a look to Riley's face in accusation.

Cade stroked the back of his hand down Riley's cheek and said, "Oh, I wouldn't be too confident of that, Brice. Ry here seems meek enough, but my girl has a competitive streak. Don't you, sweetheart?" The smile she sent him was pure mischief and Cade leaned down kiss those smiling lips before stepping back.

"Ladies," Cade said in a loud voice, "once the clamps go on, the game is on. You cannot speak unless to answer a direct question. We will use hands, mouths and toys to get the results we are after, but no cocks. That is allowed only after one of your pails is full and Riley has won."

Brice punched him good-naturedly in the arm and Terryn chuckled with a, "We'll see about that" whispered under her breath.

Hmm, seems like Riley isn't the only one with a competitive streak, Brice thought.

"To keep things fair, Trev and I will take turns with Riley," Cade continued. "Only one of us is allowed to touch her at a time."

Brice checked the rigging on Terryn's pail while Cade checked Riley's. The bungee-like cord was secured permanently to the center of the pail's handle. He made sure it was threaded properly through the pulley and then looked back at his sub. "Ladies, what are your safe words?"

"Spinach," Riley said, without taking her eyes off Cade and Trevor.

"Pickles." Brice smiled when Terryn blushed in response to the other Doms' laughter.

"Good. Use them if you have to." Then he closed the distance between him and Terryn and brushed one puckered nipple with the rubber-tipped clamp. "Ever worn clamps before, sub?"

"No, Sir." Her voice and expression showed a nice mix of fear and anticipation. Perfect.

"It's supposed to be tight. Pressure but not pinching. If it's pinching, let me know so I can adjust it." Brice waited until she nodded her assent, then squeezed the clamp and gently closed it over the rosy tip. Her gasp was breathy surprise and the sound pulsed in his gut.

"Okay?" he asked, even though he could read the answer in her face. She nodded and he clamped her other breast. He took a second to admire her this first time in clamps, then ran his hands gently down the dangling chains. He connected them to each other and then connected those to the cord of her pail. When he gave an experimental tug, Terryn let out a moan that she couldn't hold back.

"Oh, cousin," he said as he gave another tug and got another moan. "I do believe she likes these clamps."

Trevor whispered a choice cuss word at that and Brice added, "You realize this means that the more water that goes into her pail, the faster she's going to be coming."

"Don't count your orgasms yet, cuz," Cade said. "Riley, are you ready?" She bit her lip and nodded. "Terryn?" A nod from her and the game was on.

Brice wasted no time. He stepped behind Terryn and ran his open mouth along the curve of her shoulder and neck. Just as he sucked on the ultra-sensitive spot, he dipped his two longest fingers into her wet heat. Her whole body jolted and that disrupted the clamps on her breasts, bringing forth another moan and causing a mini spasm in her pussy. He nibbled and licked his way up to her ear as he kept a fast and deep rhythm with his hand.

"C'mon, Red, you are so close already. Mmmm, I can feel how close you are." He flexed those fingers to tap at her g-spot and added pressure to her clit with the heel of his hand. She let out a small cry, arched on to her toes and he could feel the climax gathering in her when he was blasted in the face with a spray of water. "Hey!"

Trevor smirked and said, "Oops." Then went back to watching Cade eating Riley's cunt.

"Fucker," he said without heat. "Another stunt like that and your poor sub gets a penalty." Then he forgot Trevor and got back to business. He could hear the wet sounds of Cade lapping at Riley and her soft sighs, and smiled. He knew Riley's sighs and she was not as close as Terryn. "Just a little more, baby, just a little and...yeah." He moaned as the buildup broke. Terryn's first climax washed over her and throbbed her flesh around his fingers in release.

"Damn it," Trevor cursed, then warned, "Brace yourself, little one." He pointed the nozzle and sprayed water into Riley's pail. She was so close to orgasm that the extra pressure hardly fazed her, though.

Brice dropped to his knees in front of Terryn and set his mouth to her. He was going to have to work fast to get her back up to the level that Riley was at, but this first win gave him hope. Terryn jolted and cried out as he whipped his tongue back on fourth on her sensitive clit, but he clamped his hands on the cheeks of her ass to hold her still. Just as the jerks of her hips subsided, showing that she was past the too sensitive stage, he heard the high cries signaling that Trevor had brought Riley to peak. He sat back and watched as Trevor carried her through the waves of it, never stopping the pumping of his hand into her until she arched and screamed again in a second climax.

"Impressive," he conceded and looked to Terryn. "That means a double portion for you, Red." Brice stepped back and reached for a hose. As the pail started to fill, Terryn's moans got louder and he couldn't help but smile. The heavier it got, the more excited she became. He looked to the others with a gloating smirk.

Cade was up again and he stepped toward Riley with one of the vibrators from the tote. Brice considered the tote for a moment, then smiled at Terryn, changed the setting on the nozzle in his hand and shot a hard stream of almost too-hot water right at her clit. With a scream, she arched on to her toes and started coming almost instantly. Not to be outdone by the likes of Trevor Wellington, Brice adjusted the setting again to pulses and continued until, sure enough, within seconds she was screaming out her own multiple orgasms. He thought he could get a third but decided to back off a little. He didn't want to get her so frazzled she called "pickles" because the game got too intense too quickly.

"Allow me," he said in false courtesy and filled Riley's pail with the appropriate amount of water. Cade and Trevor both soothed her as she panted while adjusting to the added weight. The full, ripe globes of her breasts were lifted and elongated by the time he was done. There was a pinched look around her eyes that meant the men had their work cut out for them if they were going to get her to another peak any time soon.

For the next round, he went to the tote and fished out a small vibrator and phallus. Walking back, he noticed Trevor was attaching a water willie to his hose. It was soft, had nubs all along the head and shaft and vibrated as the water shot out the end of it. It was a very effective toy. Brice wasn't daunted. What he had in store for Terryn was more than a match for that.

Her slender body was still quivering with aftershocks when he slid to his knees behind her. "Spread your legs wider for me, sub." She did with a moan. "Good girl," he praised, then said, "Now don't move."

The dildo slid into her easily, considering how wet and ready she was. She gave a grateful moan and her hips wiggled slightly. A sharp bite on her ass stopped that and he turned on the vibrator in his hand. With one hand, he spread her luscious ass and with the other he ran the vibrator along the soft outer folds of her pussy. Her hums of pleasure rocketed up to guttural shouts when he leaned forward and licked and lapped at the sweet pucker of her ass. Brice waited until she was pushing back with her hips, trying to get more of his mouth before finally bringing the vibrator to her clit.

Her scream was a flame in his blood and in that moment the game fell away and all he wanted was more. More of her ass. More of her cunt. He wanted everything she had to give and it was a hunger that wouldn't be denied. It could have been hours or minutes. Brice couldn't tell, time had stopped for him. He didn't register Riley's screams following close behind her own orgasm. Or the men switching up. He just kept going, devouring her from back to front and back again until his face was coated in Terryn's juices and her thighs were quivering against his cheeks.

As he pulled the dildo from her and stood up, he recognized the signs that not only was she in sub-space, but he had achieved top-space. That high that came when every sense was sharpened and attuned to the sub before him. Looking to the others, he realized that they too had gotten there. Riley was mindless and begging. Her hips flexed in time with her wordless pleas and her men looked like predators about to strike.

Terryn was teetering on the edge even now. Her body so primed and ready that Brice knew it would take very little to push her over again. He surmised that the others must have been keeping up with the game while he'd been lost in his sub, because the pails were both almost full. So full, in fact, that the first one to reach orgasm next would win.

He couldn't stop the taunt, didn't even want to try. "Gentlemen," he said to draw their attention. "I won."

Then he picked up a hose pointed it at those lovely, responsive breasts and blasted them. Terryn lost her mind. She shook and screamed and thrashed as he lashed those perfect tender nipples with the water. She looked breathtakingly glorious. Her pale skin was wet and glistening, her pert breasts pulled taut from her body, the nipples flushed a deep red within the clamps. As she shuddered and came in a never-ending dance of ecstasy, Brice couldn't tear his eyes away.

He didn't hear the others' applause as he dropped the hose and stalked back to her. All he heard, all he saw, was her. Wet, panting, restrained and waiting for him to take her. He dislodged the cord but left the clamps, then kissed her while he fumbled for the condom in his soaked jean pocket. He kissed her like he'd never kissed her before. Dirty and raunchy. Fucking her mouth with his the way he was going to fuck her body as soon as he got the condom on.

"Please. Please, please." It was a mantra that she breathed when he released her mouth. He got his jeans opened and was sliding the rubber in place when he heard a scream from Riley. He looked over to see her impaled by both her men—bastards didn't have to worry about condoms—with Cade in the front and Trevor taking up the rear, so to speak. The sight was electrifying and erotic. The three of them were grace and beauty together and it never left him unmoved to see them like this.

He looked back at Terryn to see her watching them and she seemed equally moved. Then he slid one of those perfect, mile-long legs of hers over his hip and drove into her with every ounce of power he had. She was screaming again. Deep guttural screams in time with the hard, driving thrusts he was pounding into her body and nothing had ever sounded or felt so good.

He gathered the chains of her breast clamps into one hand and added a rhythmic tugging to match his thrusts. She was helpless and mindless. His sub fantasies come to breathing, vivid life and in the midst of his frenzy, his heart fell.

As sure and as deep as he knew his name was Brice Marshall, he knew he was in love with the woman in his arms.

He touched his forehead to hers, gathered her closer with a hand on her ass, and said, "Come with me, baby" against her lips. "Come with me now like this. One more, c'mon...there. Like that, almost...there."

He groaned as she clenched and came in a lovely surge and he pumped once. Twice. Once more and he joined her with their heads and faces meshed together. It felt like his very soul poured into hers with every burst of release.

Chapter Seventeen

Three days later, Angie's condition was improved from critical to stable. She was still in a medically induced coma, but the doctors had hope of a full recovery. They weren't making any guarantees, but they were optimistic so it gave everyone else a reason to be hopeful too. Terryn was sitting at Angie's bedside painting her nails as she chatted about all that she'd been missing.

"Well, I for one can't wait for you to come back to work so I can quit," she told her as she brushed on a second coat of Shameless Red. "It's not that I don't love Jenny. She's awesome. I like the work too. The tips are great."

She lifted Angie's hand closer to wipe away a smudge. "I hate to say it, but it's Mandy. Wow. How you have managed to work with her for all this time, I don't know." Feeling a little guilty about talking bad about someone, even though the person she was talking to was unconscious, Terryn looked around the room before she continued.

In a much softer voice, she said, "I just started there and she's asking me what we're supposed to do. She has been there for, what? Six months? Yet she asked me how to make a vanilla latté. What's that about? How can you work at a coffee shop for six months and not know how to make a vanilla latte?"

She sighed with a shake of her head as she started on the clear coat. "It's not just that either. Have you noticed how she never really looks you in the eye?" Terryn took a few calming breaths before she said, "And the way she treats the customers. She takes forever to make a coffee and if someone makes a comment about it, she bites their head off." Terryn scooted down and started on the toes when she finished with, "I know she is sweet for the most part, but I just gotta say, I am looking forward to becoming a customer again instead of a coworker."

"When did you get here?"

Terryn startled at Jenny's voice and smeared red all over Angie's little toe.

Jenny laughed. "Oops, sorry."

"I've been here about ten minutes, why?" she asked. Jenny was looking nervously from Angie to Terryn and back again.

"Oh, I was just curious. I've been here for a while and just ran down to the gift shop for batteries. My camera is about dead." She looked at the clock and asked, "Did the nurse come in already?"

"Not since I've been here," Terryn answered.

Before she could question her about her strange behavior, Jenny spoke. "You know, I tried to fire Mandy, but she came to work anyway." Her quiet laugh was infectious and Terryn chuckled with her. "It wasn't long after she started. I told her it wasn't working out and maybe she would do better as a maid or a waitress." Jenny rolled her eyes at that and said, "Well, I took her keys and the very next day she was waiting at the back door when I pulled up to open. She said, 'I tried to get in, but you have my keys'."

With a childlike grunt of frustration, Jenny tossed her purse to the floor. The gesture was cute and disarming and Terryn laughed out loud as Jenny picked up her purse with a grimace and complained, "Who in their right mind shows up for work after they've been fired? I tried to tell her that she needed to find another job and that she didn't work here anymore and you know what she said?" Terryn shook her head and watched as Jenny's face crumpled comically into another frown and said, "'Oh, I don't need two jobs, this one is enough for me.'"

"You can't be serious?" Terryn laughed. "What did you do then?"

"What could I do? I opened up and she waltzed in and started working. She was better for a while after that, but I think I'm going to have to fire her again to keep her focused." Jenny looked as exasperated as a person could get and then reached out to brush a hand along Angie's forehead. "How are you, baby girl?"

"You didn't leave Mandy alone in the shop, did you, Jenny?" Terryn asked, just now realizing it was business hours.

"God, no." Jenny shuddered at the thought, then made a noise that could only be described as an evil chuckle and said, "Bill is there with her." And the two of them laughed like loons.

That was the sight that greeted Kent and Brice when they walked into the room. Kent asked, "You two primping my sweet girl?"

If Terryn didn't know better, she would have said that Jenny looked panicked at the sight of the two detectives.

"Are you two planning to visit long?" Her voice shook and Terryn couldn't decide if Jenny looked ready to laugh or cry when Brice answered.

"Oh, we've only got about fifteen minutes before we need to head out."

Jenny shrugged and loaded up the batteries into her digital camera and said, "Well, in for a penny, in for a pound, I guess."

Just then, the nurse walked in and Jenny snapped up her camcorder and started filming. Terryn gave her a quizzical look but held her tongue. "Angie, Doc says you are going to be okay," she narrated as she slowly panned the room before coming to rest with it pointed at the nurse.

The nurse, whose nametag read Natty, was young with dark hair and a pretty smile that she flashed to the camera as she turned back the covers. "That's right, sweetie," Nurse Natty said. "The doc will be easing back your meds in just two days and then you'll be able to turn onto your side yourself. But for now..."

She eased Angie over to her side and just as she was about to prop a pillow behind the small of her back, she stopped with a puzzled look on her face. Cautiously, she reached out and lifted the gown away from Angie's backside. Pure shock crossed her face accompanied by a gasp of outrage. The detectives and Terryn rushed to see what was wrong just as the nurse burst into hysterical laughter.

The men saw it next and Brice bent double with his hands braced on his knees as laughter boomed out of him. Kent braced himself on the mattress and laughed so hard he went silent with it. Terryn was blocked by the three so she had no idea what was going on until the nurse plopped back into a visitor chair still lost in her giggles.

Finally, Terryn got to see. She felt the punch of it hit her like a surprise even though she'd been braced to see. But there was no way to brace for this. With her expression frozen in a drop-jawed look of shock, she turned to look at Jenny and now understood why the woman had been acting so nervous.

Jenny had written on Angie's ass in big black letters when no one was looking. The words were simple and to the point.

KISS THIS.

Terryn's laughter erupted and started them all off again.

"What?" Jenny said between laughs. "She is gonna love this when she wakes up."

When Terryn got back to the shop, easygoing, smooth-tempered Bill looked fit to kill. Terryn couldn't imagine what would have put the normally smiling guy in such a foul temper. She hurried around the counter, plucked an apron off the hook that read *Muffins are like sex. Even when they aren't any good, they're still pretty good.*

She asked, "Is everything all right, Bill?"

His answer was more grunt than words, so Terryn let it go and moved to help the customer who'd just walked in. After fixing the coffee, she headed back into the kitchen for a muffin to finish the order and stumbled on what she realized must be the source of his mood. Mandy was standing way too close to Bill staring up into his face. Bill looked beyond uncomfortable and even though he was in a corner, he tried to back up even more. Terryn couldn't hear what Mandy was saying, but she didn't think Bill would mind her interruption.

"Mandy?" she said, and then repeated it louder since it didn't appear as if the woman heard her. "Did you make the peanut butter chocolate muffins this morning?"

When Mandy turned with a vacant smile and a shrug, Terryn asked, "I think those are them on the cooling rack there. Can you take them out to the counter, please? I've got to wash my hands."

Mandy smiled sweetly and shuffled over to the plates, then checked the oven. "Mandy?" Terryn said, "They're on the cooling rack."

"I know that," Mandy snapped. Her vacant pleasant face scrunched into a frown. "Who put them there?"

"I did," Bill said from his corner, giving Mandy a look.

Mandy's expression mellowed once more and she took the muffins out to the front without another word. Bill let out a gust of air that would have parted Terryn's hair had she been standing closer.

"I tell you, that woman is crazy. I don't know why Jenny keeps her on." Bill looked baffled for a moment. "The woman just has no sense of a person's personal bubble." He held a hand up in front of his face until it was almost touching his nose. "Who talks to someone this close? Who is comfortable that close unless you're getting busy?" He dropped his hand and shook his head in frustration.

"What was she talking to you about?" Terryn asked.

"She was going on and on about how much she liked Jenny, how much she liked our girls and how we were raising them right, not like some of the girls out there." He scrubbed his hands over his face as though to wash away the memory of having Mandy that close and Terryn laughed.

"Maybe you should tell Jenny she was trying to hit on you. Then Jenny would fire her for real."

Bill shrugged good-naturedly and waved that suggestion away. "Nah. You good to go here? I gotta get out of this place."

"Sure," she answered. "Mandy and I will be fine and Brice is picking me up at closing time."

Back at in the precinct, Kent was focusing on Brian and Jenny, doing some discrete digging into recent purchases and financials while Brice was trying to track down someone who had counseled Mandy in that treatment center she'd attended as a teen.

"Yes, hello," he said to the bored-sounding voice on the other end of the line. "This is Detective Brice Marshall with the NYPD. I've been trying to reach you regarding a woman you had in your care about twelve years ago?"

"Detective," the tired male voice said, "I have been here for twenty years and in those twenty years I've had no less than fifty girls a year. I certainly hope you're not expecting me to remember one of them from that far back right off the top of my head."

Alan Drake was tired. He hadn't taken a vacation in over three years and it seemed like the more he poured into the kids, the less they responded. The earnest-sounding detective kept talking and his passion for his chosen field made Alan envious. He remembered being passionate about his work.

He sighed and made a couple noncommittal sounds into the phone and looked at the pictures hanging on his wall. They were of his kids from the center over the years. Alan used to look at those photos with pride. Now he looked at them and just felt defeated. Seeing not the girls he'd helped succeed, but only the many he had never been able to reach.

It was eerie coincidence that the moment his eyes touched on Mandy, he heard her name from the eager detective. Alan sat up straight as chills raced down his spine. He stared into the vacant eyes on his wall while he listened to tales of murder.

"Detective," he interrupted, struggling not to give anything away in his voice. "You have to know I am not at liberty to say anything without a warrant."

But he wanted to, he really wanted to.

"I can get you a warrant, but girls are dying. If you know anything that pertains to this, you've got to tell me."

Alan's eyes closed, in a torment of indecision.

"I can't. I can't even acknowledge that she was here without risking my job." He stopped for a moment and added, "And I'm sure I don't need to point out what might happen to your case if the right lawyer twists around how you got your information." Alan heard the detective curse and said, "All I can tell you is please. Please get that warrant." After a beat, he said, "Hurry. I'll be waiting for your call."

Brice hung up with too much force and the sound brought several looks his way. Then Kent hung up too and the two of them said at the same time, "I think I've got something."

That gave Brice pause. "What have you got?"

Kent smiled like he was relishing what he had to say, "Bastard Brian Gwin made a little trip to the hardware store about two weeks ago and just guess what he did there?" The smile got a lot meaner. "Fucker had some keys made. How much you wanna bet one of those keys was to the coffee shop?"

Brice felt a lead ball drop in his gut at that. Kent added, "I knew there was something off about a guy that clean. No normal guy keeps his house that spotless." His brows shot up and he continued, "Makes perfect sense now. No one else on Earth coulda walked away from those scenes so clean. Had to be him. Felix fucking Unger."

"That's a pretty far stretch," Brice cautioned. "But hell, I'm game. We didn't have enough evidence to do more than a walk-through on his place the first time around. Let's see if we can get a warrant for a full search. Nobody's clean enough to fool forensics."

Kent was so excited he didn't even start whistling that stupid song like he did whenever the sexy assistant D.A. Ziporah Feldman was brought up. As he reached for the phone to call for the warrant, he stopped before dialing to ask, "Hey. What was it that you got?"

Alan had paced for an hour after pulling out Mandy Brickman's file. Then he asked his assistant to check his line and stay off the phone for the rest of the day if at all possible. Then he paced some more. After another grueling thirty minutes, a fax came through with the NYPD symbol on it. A morbid kind of excitement exhilarated him while it also saddened him.

Another hour and still no call. He checked the warrant for a call back number, but there was nothing there. The urgency was gnawing at his gut and all he could do was pace.

Chapter Eighteen

"He's not answering his phone." Brice hung up and waded through the mess the search crew was making of Brian Gwin's pristine apartment. There were white-coated technicians swarming the place and blood-revealing chemicals coating every surface. "Brian didn't show up for work today and his boss told me he had a date last night with a girl from the coffee shop next door."

Kent stood up from his search of Brian's sock drawer. "Fucker didn't take long to mourn Katie, did he?" He shook his head in disgust and resumed emptying the drawers as he asked, "So much for his big crying jag when we told him she was gone. How's the warrant for the kids' center coming? You get the news that it's through yet?"

"No," Brice said, less upset than he would have been if that were their only lead. "It should've been pushed through the same time this one was. Ziporah said she'd get them both through, so I don't know what the holdup is."

"Well..." Kent whooped and pulled a small black box from the bottom corner of the bottom drawer. "Look at what we have here. I don't know about you, Brice, but to me this looks like a goddamn souvenir stash." Then he opened the lid and cursed a blue streak as he pulled out a brand-new key that looked a lot like the ones for the deadbolt to the Surf-n-Slurp.

"Hey, you." Brian Gwin walked into the shop and smiled with surprise at Terryn. "You work here now? When did that happen?" He sauntered up to the counter and Terryn smiled back at him.

"Yes," she answered. "For a while, at least. Once the dust settles and Brice catches this guy, Jenny can hire someone else and I can go back to my girls at the rec center."

"Yeah, Katie said you were great with the girls. Even the troublemakers."

Terryn's smiled turned wistful and she watched as Mandy wiped down the glass front door and the windows on either side of it, "Yeah, there's nothing more reckless than a teenage girl with an unstable home life. It'll give a girl a wild streak, that's for sure."

Brian gave her an inscrutable look and leaned on the counter.

The search was on with renewed gusto after the box had been discovered. It held a photo of Katie and Amber together at the shop. There was a set of earrings that matched the ones Amber was wearing in the photo and a pair of skimpy pink lace panties. The lab would discover which girl those panties belonged to and now they all set themselves to finding DNA evidence with a whole new vigor so they could lock this cage once they got Brian into it.

Brice was on his cell with the precinct asking for an all points lookout for Brian as a person of interest when his other line signaled. He almost ignored it.

"Detective," Alan had said as soon as he clicked over. "I have the warrant, but you didn't call back. Have you arrested Mandy?"

Brice felt a warning tingle on the back of his neck. He stepped aside to a room that was mostly empty and answered, "No, we've got a break in the case and we're following that lead. What have you got to tell me about Mandy, Alan?"

"Oh, well," Alan hedged, "if you think you've got someone else, that would be a relief. I guess."

"It's not closed yet. If you have information that could shed some light on this, I need to hear it," he responded as that warning tingle spread from his neck to his gut.

"Mandy came to us as a teen because she'd been getting into fights at school with the other girls. Only they weren't just fights. She was ambushing girls for no apparent reason." Alan stopped and Brice could hear the shuffle of papers and surmised that the man must have been reading her file. "Three girls. All three of these girls had been brutally beaten and needed medical attention. These were vicious attacks, Detective, unwarranted, and all done in true ambush fashion. She'd hide in the alleys behind their homes and attack from behind when they walked by. Detective, when I asked her about it, her response was completely casual. She told me they were sluts and deserved what they got. She was convinced that any girl who 'put out' was worthless and needed to be put down."

Alan had stopped again and repeated himself, not realizing that Brice would be hearing those words in his nightmares for the next two weeks. "I have it here in my file. That's an actual quote from Mandy when she was little more than a child: 'Put out and get put down'."

He huffed a loud breath and finished with, "I could never reach her. She had a vacant kind of manner that made her seem disconnected from reality. Her parents were religious people, but not fanatics. They wanted their girl to wait until she married, but they were just as shocked by her actions as everyone else. Even they couldn't reach her. She just retreated behind that vacant façade and floated away whenever anyone tried to talk to her. Like we'd think she was dumb. But she was smart, Detective, smart and dedicated to the belief that she was right and any girl who had sex was worthless, damaged goods. I always thought it ironic that it was her psyche that was the damaged one."

"Kent!" he shouted after he hung up while every cell in his body vibrated in fear. "They're at the coffee shop!" And ran out the door like the fires of hell were chasing him.

Terryn was chatting away with Brian about her most challenging girls. She was leaving the names out, of course, and each story only made him laugh more as he sipped his coffee and nibbled on his muffin. With no warning his face sobered and she slowly stopped talking.

"Brian? Is something wrong?"

His expression darkened even more and he suddenly looked murderous. "What the hell?" he said, grabbing Terryn by the collar and yanking her across the counter. Over her surprised scream, she could swear she heard laughter.

Sirens blaring, Kent weaved in and out of traffic like an Indy racecar driver. Brice hung on to the dash with one hand and barked into his cell with the other. "I don't want any excuses—get every car we got out there now! The suspect is considered armed and dangerous. One-ninety, blond and blue, and don't let her fumbling manner fool you. That bitch is a stone-cold killer."

Chapter Nineteen

Brian crashed into the table with Terryn on top of him. His long arms clamped her to his chest and he yelped, "What the fuck, Mandy?"

Terryn whipped her head back to see Mandy stab into the air where she'd been standing less than two seconds ago. Then watched in horror as Mandy stalked around the counter clutching the biggest knife Terryn had ever seen. Terryn screamed and scrambled off of Brian as he lunged to his feet and shoved her behind him.

What he did next caused Mandy to laugh maniacally—he picked up a chair and pointed the legs at her like he was a lion tamer.

"Oh, that's so funny, Brian." She laughed like there was nothing wrong and she wasn't threatening them with a knife. It was eerie and caused a sweat to break out over Terryn's whole body. "Shouldn't you have a whip too?"

More creepy laughter when Brian swung it at her as she got closer. "I'm not some dumb animal." Her laughter melted away, leaving behind nothing but unmistakable madness on her face. "You won't be able to stop me with that. Nothing can stop me." Then she feinted to the left and then back to the right when he countered, and she sliced a vicious cut into his forearm. Terryn clutched at him when he staggered and yelled.

"Mandy!" Terryn barely recognized the sound of her own voice, it was so choked with fear, "Mandy, why are you doing this?"

Mandy lunged with a furious snarl at Brian's face, but he was ready this time and caught her in the stomach with the chair. She staggered back and actually pouted at him.

"Stop that," she snapped. "You don't get to hit back. Stupid, stupid, stupid boy." She opened her mouth to reprimand him more, but Brian swung the chair at her again, catching her in the face with one of the legs.

Her head snapped to the side with a nasty crunch and a spray of blood. Almost as though it was happening in slow motion, Mandy turned back to look at them with eyes that had gone flat and a smile smeared with blood. She gave him one searing glance, then looked right at Terryn as though Brian were no longer in the room.

"I'm going to kill you, slut. Kill you so you don't help any more of those little sluts at your center. And when I'm done," she continued as she slowly inched toward them again, "I'm going to kill them."

Quicker than either she or Brian could track, Mandy jumped at them with a howl of rage. They both fell under the force of the tackle. Terryn was trapped under Brian and she watched in horror as he grappled with Mandy for the knife.

Brian's shout of pain and terror turned Terryn's blood to ice. With desperate panic, she shoved out from under him in time to see Mandy's knife come down toward Brian's unprotected stomach.

Terryn didn't think—she just leaped. She barreled into the larger woman without fear for herself and a boiling rage from realizing that this was who took Katie from her. A wordless scream of vengeance spilled from her mouth as she scrambled to latch on to Mandy's knife hand.

Brice flew from the car and toward the door while his worst nightmare unfolded in front of his eyes. Brian Gwin was bleeding and struggling to get up, his focus on the fighting girls. Terryn was on top of Mandy and they both had blood on them.

Brice started praying as he pounded up to the door, only to come to a fast, hard stop as he discovered it was locked. He stepped back and pulled his gun. One shot and the shattered glass fell like rain.

"Mandy! Freeze, police!" He didn't expect it to stop them, but he couldn't get a clear shot. Terryn was smaller, but she was wrapped around the other woman like a python.

"Kent, cover me," he shouted over the girls' shrieking and reached for the knife in Mandy's hand.

Mandy saw him and flexed back out of Terryn's grasp with a violent wrench of muscle. Then she arced it forward with every intention of stabbing Terryn right in the face. Brice registered the intent and acted in the same second.

He shouted, "Now!" and instead of making a grab for the knife, he grabbed for his sub. He yanked her away from the vicious swing of that blade and the two of them crashed to the floor behind him.

The very next second, Kent fired and Mandy's chest fluttered and bloomed a sickening red.

Brice landed on his ass with Terryn gripped by her underarms. It took a while for her flight or fight frenzy to register that she was safe. She continued to struggle and scream. Eventually, the reality and terror of the moment faded away and took her energy with it like air leaving a balloon and she wilted in his arms before turning to curl in his lap.

189

"I love you." she gushed, emotions stark on her tear-ravaged face. "I was afraid I would never get to tell you that." She swallowed with a gulp and a loud sniff. "I do, though. I love you so much, Brice." Then she buried her face in his neck and bawled.

Kent kicked the knife from Mandy's grasp before turning to check on Brian. Back-up was swarming within moments, but Brice stayed on the floor. He tightened his grip on Terryn and rocked as sobs wracked her whole body. With a soft curse, he buried his face in her hair and thanked God for the phone call that had sent him here in the nick of time.

"Hey." Kent crouched down beside them and brought Brice back to the moment. "You okay?" Brice didn't trust his voice so opted to nod instead. "The paramedics are taking Brian. She got a couple good ones in. He's going to need surgery."

Brice looked over to see that Mandy was not covered in a sheet, but was also being loaded onto a gurney.

Brice grunted and lay one more kiss on the top of Terryn's head. "Red, I need you to let the paramedics check you over." He set her back from him a little and looked into her tear-soaked face.

"It was Mandy." Her bottom lip trembled and damn near broke his heart in two. "She tried to kill me and Brian dragged me over the counter." They both looked to where Brian was being loaded into the ambulance and she said, "He saved me. He shoved me behind him and used a chair to keep her away from us."

Brice and Kent shared a look and Brice realized that he was going to owe Brian a lifelong debt. "We need two crews. One to search here and another at Mandy's."

"Already on it," Kent said as he stood to let the EMT take his place so the man could check Terryn for injury. "I'll take Mandy's if you want to take over here."

Brice agreed and when the medic cleared Terryn from needing to go to the hospital, he wrapped her in his coat and tucked her into a booth. Once assured that she was taken care of, he faced the shop and the men and women that were assembled there.

"Officers," he started, "she worked here forty plus hours a week and two of the attacks took place in the alley right out back." He looked each man in the eye and finished with, "No one is leaving this building until we find the DNA needed to tie this case with a big fucking red bow."

Chapter Twenty

Two weeks later

"Man. You gotta be kidding me, dude."

Brian's baffled complaint was met with laughter. Brice, Terryn and surprisingly Kent were there to help Brian home from the hospital. Terryn had made him smile and blush when she'd waltzed into his hospital room with a bouquet of roses and announced that, as her hero, she and the detectives were going to see him home in style. In style turned out to be a limo ride to Cade's restaurant for a five-course meal followed by the three of them pitching in to help clean his place.

"Aw, c'mon, Bri," Terryn laughed and stepped into the center of the once again pristine living room. "You didn't really believe we'd make you clean up a mess like that on your first day home, did you?"

Terryn smiled as Brian slowly circled the room with jaw agape. "See, I thought it would mean more if the three of us did the cleaning ourselves." She ignored Kent's cough-covered "bullshit" and said, "But Officer Moneybags here pointed out that a neat freak like you would appreciate a professional job more."

She wasn't the least surprised or insulted when Brian nodded agreement and gave Brice a fist bump. "Good call." Then he wandered to check out the rest of his place.

"So, I gotta ask," Kent said as he picked up Brian's black box of mementos. "I know you said Katie went with you to make the key so you could help her with the after-hours deep cleaning, but...did you really do it or was that just a line to get her to go out with you?" Kent's expression made it clear which one it would have been had he been the one in that situation.

"Hey, I didn't mind." Brian looked more than a little embarrassed and also a little sad. "I like cleaning and I think I might have loved her." He shrugged and took the box with his non-bandaged hand and added, "She wasn't used to working two jobs, so the weekly deep clean was rough on her. I only did it for her twice before—well before, you know."

Terryn stepped close and looked in at Brian's keepsakes of Katie. "Oh, these were her favorites." She lifted one of the earrings up to admire. "She used to let me borrow them sometimes." Her smile was wistful as she laid it back down and ran a light finger over the picture in there. "I remember this day. Amber was wearing Katie's earrings, my blouse and a pair of Angie's boots. We teased her about the fact that she'd be walking around naked if it weren't for us."

With a sigh, she laid her head on his shoulder and whispered, "It's a nice box, Brian. It's nice that Katie was loved. I think she might've loved you too."

"So," Brice asked, "Why the other coffee shop girl?" Terryn knew that the question was a loose string that had bugged Brice for the last two weeks. She was surprised he hadn't asked it days ago.

"Oh." If anything, Brian got even redder. "You guys already think I'm too soft—this is really gonna set you off." He took a deep breath and confessed, "I don't have good medical from work." When he chanced a glance at Brice, Brice made a keep it coming gesture. "No mental health coverage or grievance counseling. Janet at the other coffee place is taking a psychology course at the community college and she agreed to talk to me. It helped to talk about her and what happened. It was deep, though. So deep I was trashed and couldn't face going to work the next day."

Kent slapped a comforting hand on his shoulder and Terryn looked at Brice with raised brows.

"Yes, Red." He answered her look with hands held up in front of him. "I'm satisfied. I'll stop." Then he wrapped his arms around her and told her, "It's over."

And it was. Mandy would not be saving the taxpayers any money. She was going to trial. Brice had assured Terryn that the ADA assigned to the case was ruthless in court. Brice wasn't worried that Mandy would ever get out of a cell, so neither was she. Although the search of the Surf-N-Slurp hadn't turned up much, Mandy's apartment had turned up blood evidence as well as a cracked and blood-encrusted bat.

"You ready to go?" Brice asked with his lips against her ear. Chills raised goose bumps up and down her arms. She nodded and she and Brice said their goodbyes and headed out. "We've got the limo to ourselves. Kent is catching a cab back to the hospital to visit Angie." Angie was awake and expected to make a full recovery. It was going to be a long, hard road for her and she'd need some restorative surgery within the next couple of months. The miracle was that there appeared to be no brain damage. Angie was as she always had been and had already charmed all her doctors and nurses.

Brice handed her into the back of the car and as soon as the door closed they were on the way.

"So where are we going in such lavish style?" Terryn snuggled her arms around him and tucked her head under his chin.

"Terryn," Brice said in that voice he used when he was in Dom mode. "Do you remember when you asked me to help you know how to be my sub?" After her whispered "Yeah," he said, "You wanted me to help you find the right balance so you'd know when to submit and how to do that without losing yourself."

She liked the sound of where this might be going and nodded with a, "Hmm-hmm."

"This is your first lesson." From out of nowhere, a small black box appeared under her nose. "We're headed to the airport. Then on to Vegas. Cade and Trevor are bringing Riley and meeting us there. And I took the liberty of calling your parents and arranging for them to meet us there as well."

She sat up and her fingers were shaking when he opened that small box to reveal a delicate antique setting surrounding a perfect square-cut diamond. "This was my grandmother's and since my father was the oldest, it went to my mother and now..." He removed it from the case and slipped it on her finger, where it fit like it was made to be there. "It goes to you."

She looked up at his face through a sheen of tears. "Terryn. I love you. I haven't said that to a woman who wasn't a relative since the third grade." When she laughed, he said in an undertone, "Pamela Sommersmith. Another redhead, but alas, she never returned my affections."

His expression grew serious again and his hands clasped hers, "I am not a man given to rash decisions. I plan out every detail and possible outcome. It's part of what makes me a good cop. But from the second I set eyes on you, everything changed. I want you for more than my sub. I want you for my wife and my partner and the mother of my children."

He brought their clasped hands to his lips and kissed her finger just above the ring. "Marry me, sub. That's an order."

Her chin quivered as love blossomed in her heart and everything that she'd been afraid to hope for since he first put cuffs on her exploded like fireworks in her soul.

Quick? Yes.

Crazy? Yes.

Was she brave enough to take this big of a gamble?

"Yes!" she yelled with a whoop and launched herself at him.

About the Author

Lainey lives in beautiful Washington State with her beloved daughter and a house full of pets. Writing is her passion and a dream that she never dared to believe could come to pass.

With the success of her first novel, *A Table for Three*, Lainey's dream became a reality. Every day she wakes up, she feels humbled and grateful for the people who helped make this possible and the readers who've been so amazingly supportive.

You can email Lainey at lainey@laineyreese.com.

Visit her website for upcoming works as well as blog posts and other tidbits at www.laineyreese.com.

Who knew snow could be so hot?

Snowfall
© *2012 Lainey Reese*

All summer long, campground manager and wilderness guide Ashley Turner dreams of the snowfall that will bring her the peace and quiet she craves. This year, though, her Cascade Mountain solitude has been threatened by too many close encounters with the local wildlife.

A huge, unusually aggressive cougar is stalking the area near her cabin, and something has to be done before someone gets hurt. But share her secluded retreat with a wildlife biologist? Though he's the perfect picture of Native American hunkiness, that's where she draws the line.

When Dr. Jake Eagle Feather shows up on her doorstep, he's prepared to call her shotgun-waving bluff. Until he can study and stop the cougar's strange behavior, she and everyone else in these snowbound mountains are in danger.

As if on cue, the cougar attacks, forcing Ashley to reluctantly give in to the inevitable. Close quarters intensify the pull of attraction between them. Even as their resistance melts in a whirlwind of sweet, hot desire, a predator is waiting out the storm for the next chance to stalk its prey…

Warning: This book contains graphic language and love scenes hot enough to melt the polar ice caps.

Available now in ebook from Samhain Publishing.

SAMHAIN
PUBLISHING

www.samhainpublishing.com

Green for the planet.
Great for your wallet.

It's all about the story...

Romance

HORROR

www.samhainpublishing.com

CPSIA information can be obtained at www.ICGtesting.com
Printed in the USA
BVOW040902070613

322731BV00003B/7/P